# WEDDING IN THE FAMILY

# Wedding in the Family

BY ROSAMOND DU JARDIN

J. B. Lippincott Company

PHILADELPHIA AND NEW YORK

# CONTENTS

*By Rosamond Du Jardin:*

WEDDING IN THE FAMILY

SENIOR PROM

THE REAL THING

SHOWBOAT SUMMER

A MAN FOR MARCY

DOUBLE FEATURE

PRACTICALLY SEVENTEEN

MARCY CATCHES UP

DOUBLE DATE

CLASS RING

WAIT FOR MARCY

BOY TROUBLE

# WEDDING IN THE FAMILY

# 1

## WEEK BEFORE THE WEDDING

MIDGE HEYDON, whose fifteenth birthday was so close behind her she could still recall the color of the candles on her cake, lay prone in the front hall, talking on the telephone. At the other end of the wire was her closest friend and practically constant companion, Judy Allen. The two had separated a scant half hour earlier, after spending most of the June afternoon playing tennis. But this lessened in no degree the number of things they had to say to each other, or the immediacy of their need to say them. Midge's mother had once remarked that if all the words the two girls had exchanged could be preserved and bound, they'd fill as many volumes as an encyclopedia. And her father, whose sense of humor was unfailing, if a shade corny, had answered that you couldn't bind hot air in book covers, but that possibly the air force could utilize it to float a weather balloon.

Midge didn't mind this sort of good-natured kidding. For one thing, as the youngest of four sisters, she was used to it. And for another, she felt that there were limits to what a pair of parents could be expected to take. In Midge's considered opinion, if they weren't permitted the safety valve of ribbing their offspring occasionally, they might blow their stacks in ways that were infinitely harder to cope with.

She hunched herself into a more comfortable position, propping her bare feet on the second step of the stairs and elbowing one of her kicked-off loafers out of the way. As she and Judy talked on animatedly, skipping from one fascinating topic to another, Midge began to feel both hungry and thirsty, sensations which overwhelmed her frequently and with such force that it was unthinkable to ignore them.

"Hey!" she exclaimed. "I'm starving. Hang on a sec."

"Me, too," Judy concurred. "Be right back."

Midge put down the phone and rushed kitchenward, a tall, slim, agile figure, whose crumpled white shorts left her deeply-tanned legs bare and whose red-blond hair was pulled back from her face and tied with an aqua silk scarf into a bouncing pony-tail. Her striped tee shirt hung loose and shapeless in the accepted fashion, but beneath it were indications of a nicely developing figure, which Midge, dazzled by the overblown beauties of Hollywood, considered woefully inadequate.

The large kitchen was empty, cool and with a between-meals orderliness. A breeze spiced by the scent of mock orange billowed the crisp white curtains with their bright gingham top ruffes and tiebacks. The tiled floor felt cool beneath Midge's feet as she plopped acros it to the over-sized refrigerator. She proceeded too pen this and extract from it a bottle of root beer, several ripe olives, a bunch of grapes and a cold chicken leg left from last night's dinner. The cookie jar tempted her from the cabinet, so she took a handful of brownies and returned to the hall.

Here she sat on the bottom step of the stairway, with her snack apportioned between her free hand and her paper-napkin-spread lap and picked up the phone.

Her "Hi?" into the mouthpiece was questioning.

Only silence greeted her. Judy wasn't back yet. Midge ate a couple of olives, bit into her chicken leg and took a long refreshing swig of root beer before Judy's breathless "Hi" reached her ears.

"Slow-poke!" Midge accused.

"I got sidetracked," Judy explained. "The paper boy came and instead of it just being Jack Finley it was his older brother, Mart—you know, the one that goes to military school and has a butch haircut and big ears."

"Oh, him," Midge said with no particular enthusiasm. "So of course you had to take in the paper before he got away instead of just letting it lie there as usual. His ears aren't so big you wouldn't do that, at least."

Judy giggled. "Well, natch! Wouldn't you?"

"Yep," Midge admitted, laughing, too. "Only he's already been here. I heard the paper thud on the porch when we first started talking. How come he's taking Jack's route?"

"Jack has poison ivy," Judy explained. "And Mart hasn't got a regular summer job yet, so he's helping Jack out till the itching lets up. It's so hot, I offered him a drink of ice water and he seemed real grateful. He's got a kind of cute grin. Did you ever notice?"

"As a matter of fact, no," Midge said thoughtfully. "But then, I haven't actually seen him this summer. And of course he was away at school all winter. And way back before that, I wasn't as interested in the opposite sex as

I seem to be these days. Maybe I'd better take a good look at him when he brings tomorrow's paper. How tall is he?"

"Oh, not so very," Judy admitted. "Five-seven or eight."

"You can have him," Midge said generously. "I'm nearly that tall myself. I've decided," she went on, her voice slightly muffled with chicken, "that I'm never going to date a single man in my whole entire life who isn't at *least* six feet tall in his socks."

"Why," her friend demanded, "in his socks? He'd wear his shoes when he dated you, wouldn't he?"

"Okay, funny girl," Midge drawled. "That's the way it always is in books. The hero is never less than six feet tall in his socks. It's practically a tradition, like smoking a pipe and being brave and broad-shouldered and—"

"You and your books," Judy interrupted. "If you ask me, all that reading you do gives you some very strange ideas. Hardly any boy our age is six feet tall and you know it. You have to be realistic!"

"Oh, I don't mean just unimportant little dates exactly," Midge backed down a bit. "But I never intend to get seriously interested in a man who isn't—"

"Who wants to get serious?" Judy broke in airily. "I don't! I just want to have fun and meet loads of boys and have millions of dates for years and years and years."

"Well, so do I," Midge admitted with a little laugh. "But, after all, we're practically certain to get serious about somebody eventually. And when that time comes, he'll have to be at least six feet tall. After all, it wouldn't be any fun to have a husband I couldn't look up to."

They were off on their favorite topic—boys, past, present and future. Boys they knew. Boys they didn't know. Boys they might someday meet. Specific boys, or just boys in general. It was an ever-fascinating subject. The fact that neither of them had had more than a dozen real dates in her life didn't serve to dull their vital interest in the male sex in the slightest degree. Midge and Judy could—and had been known to—carry on a conversation about boys for as long as they were permitted by their families to hang onto the telephone. But today there was an interruption.

Midge's sister, Tobey, arrived home from a shopping trip, laden with intriguing packages and wearing the gently smiling, dreamy-eyed, slightly-detached-from-the-world look of a girl whose wedding looms only seven exciting days away. Tobey had always been Midge's favorite sister and although she had been away at college the greater part of the past four years, the closeness and understanding between them had survived their separation, just as it had survived the considerable difference in their ages. Midge thought that Tobey was the prettiest and cleverest and most wonderful girl she knew. Not that she would have thought of admitting it out loud.

Now she said, attracting Tobey's attention in the rather dim hallway, "Hi."

"Oh, hi," Tobey said, her smile widening. "It's so bright outside, I didn't see you." Then she asked, staring harder, "What are you doing, having a picnic?"

Midge laughed. "Just a snack, while I talk to Judy." She explained into the phone then, "It's Tobey—she just got home. Hang on." She inquired, her eyes on Tobey's double armload of bags and boxes, "What you got?"

"Oh, things and stuff," Tobey said. "Some blouses and lingerie and the darlingest copper-bottomed skillet and some bath towels—" she broke off, "You can see them all later when you're through talking. Is Mom home yet?"

Midge shook her head. "She had about a million errands to do. Want a brownie?"

Tobey said, "Bring some up to my room later. I haven't got a free hand right now. And a Coke, if you don't mind." She went on past Midge and up the stairs.

Midge watched her go until Judy's voice saying, "Midge?" recaptured her attention.

"Yeah," she murmured into the phone. "I can't talk much longer. Tobey's got a whole stack of the most fascinating-looking packages. I'm dying to see what she bought."

Judy sighed enviously. "It must be such *fun* having a wedding in the family. I just love weddings!"

"So do I," Midge admitted dreamily. "And it's not only the wedding itself that's going to be so exciting. Every day just stacks of presents come. And starting next week the house will be simply popping with people. My oldest sister, Janet, and husband and kids are coming from California. And Tobey's out-of-town bridesmaids will be getting here and there'll be all sorts of parties and dinners and things. I can hardly wait!"

"Lucky," Judy moaned. "Do you realize I'll never be involved in anything like that in my whole life, because I haven't any sisters? And when my brother gets married, if he ever does, it'll be his girl's family that has all the fun—not us. It's just not fair!"

"Well, there'll be your own wedding," Midge tried to cheer her, although that seemed a very long way off.

"But it won't be the same," Judy insisted dramatically, "because then I'll be all emotionally involved and not able to just sit on the sidelines enjoying it."

"Yeah, I guess that's right," Midge had to admit. "I do have a sort of box seat for the whole show, when you get right down to it."

"Sure, you do," Judy said. "You'll get to see everything and go to everything. And then as the absolute climax, you'll be wearing that perfectly delectable green dress and being a bridesmaid. Some people," she complained, "get all the breaks."

"Well, anyway, you're invited to the wedding," Midge reminded, but even as she said it, she realized that wasn't too much comfort.

Everything Judy had said was true. The preparations and preliminaries were nearly as exciting as the ceremony itself and they lasted a lot longer. For weeks, ever since Tobey's graduation at the end of May, the entire Heydon household had been in a bubbling stew of activity. And the closer it got to the twenty-seventh of June, the more enjoyable it all became. And here she was, lucky Midge, right in the thick of it. No wonder poor Judy was envious.

Tobey's wedding would be wonderful, Midge knew. Because now she was grown up and could actually take a full part in the pre-wedding festivities. Something wonderful would be going on almost every day next week, all building up to the crashing climax of the wedding itself on Friday evening.

"Promise me," Judy was saying, "that you'll remember every single detail of everything that happens—all the parties and stuff and what people say to you and whether anything fabulous happens, like meeting some exciting new boys and—well, everything, so that you can tell it all to me!"

"Of course I will," Midge assured her solemnly. "I'll tell you everything that happens. I'd never hold out on you, Judy."

"Well, okay," her friend said, sounding a trifle happier, at least. "That'll be the next best thing to me being in on it all myself."

But it wouldn't be the same, Midge knew, feeling a qualm of sympathy. Second-hand was never as good as first-hand.

But I'll be right there in the midst of everything, she thought ecstatically. I won't miss a thing.

She felt so happy, she could scarcely bear it.

# 2

## TALK WITH TOBEY

TOBEY'S DOOR was open when Midge carried up a Coke and a handful of cookies a few minutes later. And Tobey stood at the mirrored door of her closet, holding up to her shoulders a sheer white blouse with lacy ruffles spilling down the front. Tobey, Midge thought, was so beautiful these days. Happiness seemed to shine out from within her, making her coppery hair more gleaming, her brown eyes brighter, her smile warmer than ever before.

She smiled now, her glance questioning as it met Midge's in the mirror, and asked, "You like it?"

Midge breathed, "It's darling! All those little ruffles!"

Tobey said, "It's one of those drip-dry deals, or I wouldn't have got it. Not for me to iron! I expect to have a hard enough time coping with shirts."

Midge wiped her fingers idly on the sides of her shorts. The thought of Tobey, in a little apartment, doing the laundry and housework for Brose Gilman and herself, struck Midge, as always, with a slight jolt. It just didn't seem possible that by the end of next week Tobey would be Mrs. Ambrose Gilman and not Tobey Heydon at all! That was the only part of the wedding Midge really dreaded, losing her sister. Tobey and Brose wouldn't even be living in Edgewood any more. Midge felt lost and empty whenever the thought occurred to her.

Brose, who had majored in chemistry at college, had an instructorship entailing the opportunity to do graduate work in research at Midwestern University. And Tobey had lined up a job in the university library, so they would be setting up housekeeping in a campus apartment as soon as they got back from their honeymoon. It would seem so queer, Midge reflected glumly, to be the only Heydon daughter left at home. Why, with just Mom and Dad and her living in the whole big old house, they'd positively rattle around. And she was going to be sunk without Tobey to tell things to and ask for advice and get ideas from.

"Darn it!" she exclaimed aloud, her face suddenly woebegone. "I'm going to miss you!"

"Now what brought that on?" Tobey's tone was gently teasing. "Here we are, talking about my new blouse and you go off on a complete tangent."

"It was what you said about ironing," Midge explained. "And then I got to thinking about your living so far away I'll practically never see you."

"It won't be that bad," Tobey told her. "But I'll miss you, too. Of course, we were apart all the time I was at college. But it was fun seeing how you'd changed and grown up a little more each time I got back for vacations."

"How will I get along without you to hash things over with?" Midge brooded.

"You'll do just fine," Tobey assured her. "After all,

you won't be needing so much advice about boys from me, now that you're fifteen."

"But I will," Midge insisted. "I don't really know very much about them at all yet."

"You'll have a lot of fun finding out for yourself." Tobey set her empty bottle on the dresser with a little smile. "I did." She turned back toward the bed then and picked up a white-and-silver-striped box. "Wait till you see the slip I bought. Oh, and I found just the color bath towels I've been looking for. It was really quite a successful shopping trip. I even bought something for you."

"Did you?" Midge asked delightedly. "What?"

"It's here somewhere." Tobey was rummaging among bags and boxes. "Here it is," she said, pulling a green bag toward her. "I've been so sick of seeing that mangy-looking pink critter you keep on your bed, I thought if I got you a replacement maybe you'd throw the old one out. There, see?" She took from the bag a miniature stuffed tiger, green glass eyes gleaming, eyebrows quirked quizzically, yellow-and-black-and-white striped body curled in a comfortably reclining position. "Isn't he cute?"

"Oh, Tobey," Midge reached out for the toy, her eyes lighting, "he's just darling! How did you know I've been wanting one of these for ages?"

"I must be psychic." Tobey grinned. "Actually, I sort of fell for him myself, he has such a beguiling expression. Now will you throw out that messy pink dog you've had practically forever?"

"Poor old Pootsie?" Midge demurred. "After all these years of faithful service?"

"Okay, okay," Tobey said drily. "But at least put it away in a closet somewhere, so your room won't look so awful."

"Will do," Midge agreed. She smoothed the tiger's head thoughtfully. "Wonder what I should name him? Something real tigerish like—well, maybe Boo, because tigers are so scary?"

Tobey laughed. "He doesn't look scary, really. But Boo would be cute."

"Okay, Boo," Midge addressed the toy tiger solemnly. "That's your name now, remember?" Her glance lifted to Tobey. "Thanks a million for getting him for me."

"That's all right," Tobey told her.

They examined the rest of her purchases, the older girl displaying them and the younger exclaiming over them with equal enjoyment. Clothes for her trousseau, aqua bath towels with a tiny gold thread, a shining copper-bottomed frying pan, all these were part of the new life Tobey was so soon to embark upon. Midge sat holding the frying pan, feeling its cool smoothness with her palms, thinking of Tobey's marriage, of her being Brose's wife, wondering and feeling thrilled and not knowing the words to put her thoughts into.

Tobey must have sensed something of her sister's groping uncertainty, because she said, her voice quiet and more serious than usual, "I suppose it seems strange to you to think of me going away with Brose, of our being married and my leaving all of you. I know I'll miss you—

but—well, it's just that this is the next step in my life and I have to take it. And I know it's so right, our marrying. I've been sure Brose was the one for such a long while."

"But how?" Midge asked. "How can you tell when someone's the right one? Are there any—well, rules, any way you can be absolutely certain?"

Tobey's smile was gentle. "I don't know about rules, I never heard of any. When Brose and I finished high school," she went on, "we were pretty sure we were in love. But we both wanted to be positive we weren't just a sort of habit with each other, so we went to different colleges and dated lots of people and gave ourselves time to grow up, so that we could understand ourselves and each other better and find out whether we wanted the same things out of life."

"But you didn't change really, did you?" Midge asked. "I mean you went on feeling just the same way."

"Well, not exactly," Tobey admitted. "It's—sort of hard to explain. But it seems that as we grew older the way we felt about each other grew, too. Now it has a real solid foundation under it and doesn't just rest on the fact that we enjoy kissing each other and dancing together and that we find the other attractive looking and all that. Such things still enter into it, of course, but there's so much more. There's—well, just the happy feeling we get from being together. Each of us feels incomplete without the other. I guess that's what marriage is, really—a bringing together of two parts and making something out of them that's a lot bigger and stronger and more vital than either of them could ever be alone."

Midge nodded. She felt proud and happy to have Tobey talk to her like this, as if they were contemporaries, as though she were grown up, too. She asked, "Wasn't it awful for you, though, being apart so much while you were in college and growing surer all the time that you really loved each other?"

"It was," Tobey admitted. "And the fact that Brose is a horrible letter writer didn't help a bit. Of course, there were summers. But we've missed each other so much this year, since we got engaged last August—well, I wouldn't want to go through it again, I can tell you! Of course, we knew we were being sensible, finishing school first. But it isn't always the easiest thing in the world to be sensible. And what made the situation really tough was the fact that we both knew, if Brose was going to get anywhere in chemistry, he'd have to go on to graduate school." She admitted, smiling, "This instructorship Midwestern offered him really fixed us up, otherwise I don't know what we'd have done."

"But won't you mind having to work and keep house, both?" Midge asked. "That isn't going to be so easy."

Tobey shook her head firmly. "I don't mind a bit. It's going to be wonderful, being able to earn a salary and help out with our expenses, so we can get started off right." She told Midge then, her brown glance thoughtful, "Maybe there is a rule about how you can tell you're really in love. If you have an urge to do all you can for the other person, to go more than just halfway in your relationship, if what you can do for him seems more important to you than what you want him to do for you—well, that's the real thing." She laughed then and laid her hand lightly, affectionately on Midge's shoulder. "And that, my dear sister, ends our lesson for today. How did we ever get so all-fired serious, I wonder?"

Midge smiled, too, but her tone was solemn. "I'm glad we did," she told Tobey. "We won't have too many more chances to talk—really talk. I mean, next week when Janet and all of them get here and the house is full of bridesmaids and wedding guests and everybody—well, I'm glad you told me about things today."

Their eyes met in a look of understanding. Then Midge asked, "Want me to help you put any of this stuff away?"

"Not right now," Tobey said. "First I'm going to change my dress and get out of these heels."

As she turned toward the closet, the phone rang and Midge said, "It's probably Judy again," and scooted downstairs to answer it.

But it was Brose Gilman's voice at the other end of the wire. "Hi, future sister. Is my beautiful bride-to-be back from her shopping spree?"

"Um-hum," Midge said. She held the phone against her shoulder to call upstairs, "Tobey, it's Brose."

"Tell him to hang on." Tobey's voice sounded muffled, as though she might be pulling a dress over her head.

"She'll be down in a minute," Midge said. "If you've got any terribly vital and exciting news, you can tell me."

"Oh, I can, can I?" Brose chuckled. "And just what would you consider terribly vital and exciting? How about the fact that my best man just wired me that he's

going to be able to get here the first of the week, in time
for all the parties and festivities after all?"

"Is he really?" Midge exclaimed. "Your roommate at
college? The one from Texas?"

"None other," Brose said.

"The one that's tall, dark and terrific and that all the
girls go mad over? Johnnie something—what's his
name?"

"Down, girl," Brose laughed. "He's an old man my
age, a doddering twenty-two. But your description fits
him perfectly. And 'the name's Randall, of the San
Antonio Randalls,' to quote Johnnie. Nothing so vulgar
as oil wells in their background, just a little block or two
of real estate—in downtown San Antonio, of course.
He's quite a guy."

"Okay, I'm here now," Tobey said, swooping down the
stairs, reaching out eagerly for the telephone.

Midge handed it over and headed up toward her own
room as Tobey and Brose began talking. Her thoughts
were stirring excitedly. Johnnie Randall did sound like
quite a person, even if Brose was stringing her along a
little bit. Of course, he was pretty old. Too old, Midge
reminded herself, to pay the least bit of attention to her.
That was the trouble with being the very youngest
member of a wedding party. Everyone was years too old
to pay any attention to her. "Oh, well—" she murmured
aloud philosophically as she opened the door of her
bedroom.

It was in its customary state of untidiness, clothes
tossed about, the desk a shambles of stationery and
books. Lived-in was the way Midge preferred to describe

it, and the mad confusion didn't bother her a bit. But now, looking around with eyes unaccustomedly critical, it struck her that the whole room seemed pretty childish, with its flowered chintz bedspread and matching café curtains, its fluffy pink scatter rugs. And old Pootsie there on the bed, limp and soiled and missing one eye—he supplied the final infantile touch. Why, she'd had Pootsie since she was eight years old, Midge remembered with horror. She used to sleep with her arm around him when she felt a little scared in the dark.

Distastefully, she picked up the ancient toy by one ear and tossed it into the wastebasket, then went back to Tobey's room and got the lovely new stuffed tiger. She installed Boo in the middle of her pillows and stood back to study the effect. But it wasn't right at all. Yellow-and-black-and-white stripes simply didn't go well with pink flowered chintz. Boo looked smart and sophisticated, making everything else in the room seem even more childish by comparison. Maybe, Midge thought, when the wedding was over and things had settled back to normal, she could talk her parents into redecorating her room. Maybe she could fix it up like a sitting room rather than just a bedroom, with some sort of splashy abstract print in the curtains and perhaps a black corduroy spread, so that the bed would look more like a couch.

Suddenly Midge noticed Pootsie, his one eye fixed reproachfully on her from the wastebasket. True, he was old and beat-up, but somehow she felt a qualm at the thought of really discarding him. Impulsively she went over and retrieved him, then stood with him in her hands for a moment. He felt soft and squishy and familiar. Midge laid her cheek fleetingly against his pink head before stowing him away back out of sight on her top closet shelf.

# 3

## AUNT MIDGE

O N MONDAY Midge went with the rest of the family to meet Janet and Jim and their two little boys when they arrived from California. The station platform was practically overrun with Heydons, waiting for the train to get in. Mom and Dad were there, of course, and Tobey, accompanied, as usual, by Brose. Alicia Wentworth, the other Heydon daughter, had come along, too. She and her husband, Adam, were living in the big Wentworth house with Adam's father, who owned the town's largest department store. Adam, recently finished with his medical studies, was serving his internship at the Edgewood Hospital, so he hadn't been able to get away. Alicia, who was seven months pregnant, looked rather pale, but pretty, in a mint-green maternity frock, her ash-blond hair short and curly around her face. As was to be expected with Alicia's personality, she had everyone fussing over her, finding her a seat and asking if she wasn't too warm and bringing her a drink of water. Trust Alicia, Midge thought with good-natured indulgence, to take full advantage of her condition and the privilege it gave her of being the center of attention. If Adam were around, she'd be acting even more fragile and helpless.

27

It seemed the train would never arrive, but it finally did. Only fifteen minutes late, too, which was pretty good for Edgewood. Five-year-old Stevie and eight-year-old Jimmy were the first passengers off, right behind the conductor. And Janet and Jim, looking a little weary after their flight from the coast and the train trip from Chicago, were close behind them. Jimmy and Stevie were obviously still going strong. They were tanned, healthy, butch-cut and bouncing with energy. Janet was pencil-slim and stunning in a beige shantung suit, her auburn hair done in a smooth chignon at the nape of her neck. And Jim was his usual big, dark, easygoing self.

Just at first the boys seemed a bit overwhelmed with all the kissing and embracing and exclaiming. After all, they hadn't seen their mother's family in quite a long while. But the strangeness wore off quickly and they began spouting all the fascinating details of their trip; how the stewardess had let them take a peek at the pilots flying the plane; how a lady had been sick in a paper bag; how they had seen clouds from up above and the snow-caps on the tippy-tops of the mountains. Both of them talked at once and so continuously it became difficult for the grownups to get a word in edgewise.

"Hey, break it up, fellas," Jim said finally. "You can tell grandma and grandpa all that stuff later. You're drowning everybody out."

"Why don't we go home?" Dad suggested. "We can sit down and talk there."

And Mom seconded, "I've got a sandwich lunch all ready. And then I expect you'll want to rest, after that long trip."

"Rest?" young Stevie exclaimed in an appalled tone. "I been restin' all the way from home."

It was on a wave of laughter at his remark that they went out and piled into the two cars, the Heydons' sedan and Alicia's green convertible, that waited at the curb. Later, over lunch on the shaded side porch, with the boys happily picnicking under a tree in the big yard, they had a chance really to talk. All the loose ends got tied up, all the questions about the wedding were asked and answered, all the interesting family news related. Gradually everyone settled back into the easy relationship of old times when they had not lived so far apart and had been able to see each other more often.

Midge found her first feeling of strangeness with her oldest sister and her family floating away on the tide of lively talk and laughter. She had never, really, had much chance to get acquainted with Janet's children. Jimmy, whom they used to call Toots, had been only three when big Jim's job as an engineer took them all out to the west coast. And little Stevie had been born out there. Midge's only contact with him had been during a two-weeks' visit she and Tobey and their parents had made to California two years ago. That had been such a whirl of sight-seeing and gay activity, it hadn't left much time for anything else. Midge hoped it wouldn't be that way now. But with the wedding and all its attendant festivities, she was afraid there wouldn't be much time for getting to know each other now, either. It was a shame, she reflected, when families had to live so far apart.

As though Tobey's thoughts must have paralleled her own, Midge heard her sister say, "I wish you didn't live so far away! We always have such fun when we're together."

"I know," Janet agreed. "But I guess we should feel lucky we're all in the United States, at least. One of Jim's engineer friends just took off for Bangkok."

"Remember," Midge remarked, "when you went with Jim to Central America and we kept Jimmy for you?"

"How could I forget it?" Janet said, smiling. "I made a deal with Tobey to write me weekly letters about him and all I got was a blow-by-blow description of her love life with maybe a couple of lines about Jimmy in the postscript. And she charged me a dollar a week, too."

"What a fiend I must have been." Tobey shook her head. "Mercenary, too."

But however many detours the conversation took, it always seemed to get back to the wedding. "Tell me," Janet asked, "just what this week's schedule is. I hope I brought the right clothes for everything."

"If you'd brought any more," Jim cracked drily, "the plane couldn't have carried enough fuel for the trip."

"Well," Tobey enumerated on her fingers, "there's a hen party at Kay Lamb's tonight, which may turn out to be a shower, I suspect. Tomorrow Brose's best man will get here from Texas and the Gilmans are having a dinner party. Wednesday's Alicia's and Adam's party for us at the country club. Thursday's rehearsal—Barb and Suz, my other two attendants will be here by then—"

"Wait a minute," Janet interrupted. "Don't the Walters live right in the next block? How come Barb isn't around?"

"Oh, they moved to Florida over a year ago," Tobey

explained. "Didn't I tell you in my letters? I haven't seen Barb since, but, of course, we write. And I just couldn't get married without her being a bridesmaid. We've had that all fixed up ever since our junior-high days. It's a shame she can't get here in time for Alicia's party, too, but she just couldn't make it."

"And Suz is a friend from college?" Janet queried.

Tobey nodded. "My very best friend there. You'll love Suz. She was just married a few weeks ago, at the college chapel. She and Denny will be stopping here on their way back from their own honeymoon. They met at college, you know. He was an instructor there for a while, until he got his master's and landed a better job. And I sort of had a hand in their starting to date. I suppose that's one reason I get such a bang out of their marrying."

"Anyway," Tobey went on, "after the rehearsal Thursday evening Mom and Dad are having a buffet supper for the Gilmans and us and all the bridal attendants. And then Friday—well, there's just the wedding."

Her laughing glance met Brose's as she finished and Midge could see him squeeze her hand. The look on their faces made her feel all warm and stirred up inside.

"If," Brose said drily, "anybody's left alive by then after such a week."

But his eyes said something quite different. Midge drew a deep breath and exhaled it in a soft long sigh and wondered whether anyone would ever look at her like that—anyone any time during her whole life . . .

Midge had just finished helping Mom with the lunch dishes when there was a knock at the back screen door and she looked around to see Bob Pierson's familiar face and angular form framed in the aperture. Bob had blue eyes, close-cut brown hair and a grin that some of the girls at school considered quite attractive. But he was only an inch or so taller than Midge and she had known him forever, so the sight of him had little effect on her.

"Hi," he greeted in his new, deep voice to which she was not yet accustomed, having heard him speak in a higher pitch during the long years of their childhood. "Want to go swimming?"

"Oh, gee, Bob, I don't think so." Midge shook her head.

"Swimming?" Jimmy's voice said shrilly from behind her. "Golly Moses, let's! It's so hot I'm dying!"

And Stevie echoed, "Yeah, let's! Somebody around here got a pool?"

Bob peered, frowning, through the screen door, and Midge explained, "These are my nephews, Bob. Stevie and Jimmy Clark."

"Yeah," Jimmy said. "And she's our Aunt Midge."

"Aunt Midge," Stevie echoed, nodding vehemently.

Bob chuckled. "Aunt Midge—that's a new one."

Mom, on her way out of the kitchen, laughed from the doorway, "She doesn't seem exactly the aunt type, does she, Bob?"

But the little boys had no intention of being sidetracked. Jimmy asked, "Where you going to take us swimming?"

"There's only the town pool," Midge said a trifle tartly. "And he didn't ask you; he asked me."

"Well, Golly Moses." Jimmy's tone was affronted.

"I guess if it's a public pool anybody can swim in it, can't they?"

"Yeah, can't they?" Stevie echoed plaintively.

"But, boys," Mom interposed, her sympathetic glance seeking Midge's, "you just don't understand. We'll do something else that's fun."

Stevie and Jimmy looked utterly stricken, their piteous glances going from Mom to Midge.

"Anyway," Midge said, feeling like a fiend in human form, "I'm not even going."

Bob spoke casually, his glance, too, seeking Midge. "Heck, we could take them along if they want to go that bad, couldn't we?"

Midge opened her mouth to speak, but before the words could emerge, she heard Janet, who had been drawn out to the kitchen by all the voices, inquiring, "Take them along where?"

"Swimming," Midge started to explain, "but—"

"Oh, wonderful!" Janet said. "They're both regular fish and they love the water. You won't have to worry about them a bit. If, that is," she added hopefully, "you're sure you two wouldn't mind their trailing along?"

So Midge found herself spending the afternoon at the crowded pool after all. Its official name was the Edgewood Community Pool, but it was referred to laughingly as the community bathtub, so great was its customary congestion. This didn't bother Jimmy and Stevie a bit, but Midge, after a couple of dives and a few stormy crossings, bumping into or being bumped into by someone every few feet, gave up and stretched out in the sun, safely back from the water's edge. Pretty soon Bob, tanned and dripping in his yellow trunks, came and sat down beside her.

"What a rat race," he said.

Midge nodded. "But it was your idea. I'm the one who got roped in."

Bob grinned. "Anyway, it gave you a chance to show off that new bathing suit."

True, her white suit was new, but Midge was surprised Bob had noticed. She said, "I've really been saving it for when we get up to our cottage at Green Lake next month. That's where the swimming's terrific!"

"How long will you be there?" Bob asked.

"The whole month of July, the same as always. Judy's coming up to the lake with me," Midge added. "That'll make it even more fun."

Bob flopped over on his stomach beside her, leaning his chin on his cupped hands. "While you two are swimming in that nice cool lake every day, you can think of me back here working."

"You've got a job?" Midge asked in surprise.

"Yard work," Bob said. "Me and my trusty gasoline mower. Oh, and I clip hedges, too, and stuff like that."

"How come? You never worked summers before."

"I'm a big boy now," he said and grinned. Then he said, sobering, "I've got to earn some dough."

"What for?" Midge pressed curiously.

"A car," he confided.

"You're kidding! You're not old enough to get your driver's license yet."

"I know," Bob said. "But by the time I am, I aim to have a car all set and ready. Get me a good old timer, that's what I want to do, and take her all apart and put her together so she runs real sweet." His tone was soft and warm with enthusiasm, in a way Midge had never heard it before. Why, that was the way a boy's voice should sound when he was talking about a girl, only it never seemed to, at least in Midge's limited experience.

Her heart beat a little faster at the thought of how it would be to have Bob speak of her in that enthralled way. Not that he ever would, Midge reminded herself. Not that she'd even want him to. Not old Bob, who meant nothing at all to her, really.

Cold water dripped on Midge's sun-warmed legs and she winced as Jimmy's teasing voice demanded from behind her, "What you two doing up here? The water's keen!"

"The water's okay." Bob grinned at him. "There just isn't enough of it to go around, so we thought we'd let somebody else use our half gallon of it."

Midge laughed and Jimmy frowned. "Sure, there's enough to go round," he argued. Apparently he suspected he was being kidded, but wasn't quite certain how to respond. Then he shrugged, one of those all-older-people-are-nuts sort of shrugs, and asked hopefully, "Want to see me dive? I can almost do a jackknife, honest! Want to see me?"

"Sure," Bob said. "We'd love to see you. Go ahead."

"Watch now!" Jimmy called shrilly across his shoulder as he headed for the diving platform.

Midge and Bob watched as he climbed to the lowest board and plummeted off in a dive unlike anything either of them had ever seen before. Stevie stood nearby, wide-eyed with admiration.

"So that's almost a jackknife." Bob chuckled. But he lifted his hands and made an applauding sort of motion as Jimmy came up sputtering and glanced toward them expectantly.

"You know what?" Midge asked suddenly.

Bob shook his head.

"It just struck me what we're doing," she said.

"What?" Bob queried.

"Baby-sitting," Midge answered drily.

# 4

## NARROW ESCAPE

THE HEN party at Kay Lamb's did turn out to be a shower. Tobey had been quite correct in her suspicion, although she did an excellent imitation of a girl being completely surprised. The gifts ranged from personal things, filmy slips and lacy nighties, to cooking utensils and clever kitchen gadgets. Midge watched each colorful package being opened with almost as much delighted anticipation as did Tobey. She experienced a vicarious thrill, too, at the beauty of the table decorations, all pink and white, with tiny paper parasols attached to the place cards and a cake abloom with extravagant sugar roses.

After the refreshments they played a few games, in between bursts of the lively chatter and laughter that always seemed to accompany showers. It made Midge feel grown-up and important to be a part of it all, even if some of Tobey's friends did talk to her as though she were about twelve years old, asking her how she liked school and other equally stupid questions. She liked school fine, although it wasn't a thing you'd come right out and admit in public. Why was it, Midge pondered, as the talk ebbed and flowed about her like a frothy sea, that you always felt you had to tone down the fact that you enjoyed your studies and got better than average grades? Of course, to stress the point unduly might sound like bragging. Still, it wasn't exactly shameful, although the way you had to keep it a secret it seemed so.

The thing was, people always assumed that if you liked school and didn't actually mind studying, you didn't like anything else. But that wasn't the case at all! She was mad about horseback riding. She loved dancing and swimming and tennis and ever so many other sports. And she was vastly interested in and tremendously curious about boys. She meant to learn a lot more about them during the next few years, too, and find out what really made them tick, so that she could be happily at ease with them, as Tobey always seemed.

Why, Midge reflected, a girl should be able to learn a little more about the male sex from every boy with whom she came in contact. Even old Bob. She had proved that to her own satisfaction this afternoon. Just as an experiment, she had followed the advice she had read and heard so often, to find out what a boy was truly interested in and encourage him to talk about it. In Bob's case that was cars and when she'd asked him a few questions on the subject, she'd hardly had to bother to say a word all the rest of their time together. She had simply listened and put in an "Is that right?" or "I never realized that" now and then and he had seemed to have a perfectly wonderful time. She had had more fun than usual, too, since Bob wasn't always so talkative.

"What are you sitting there thinking about so seriously?" Janet asked and Midge started slightly.

"Boys," she admitted after a second's hesitation.

Her sister's smile was warmly affectionate. "Well, that's fascinating food for thought." She shook her head then. "I just can't get over your being so grown-up, though. Why, when you came out to visit us, you were only a child. A few years make such a difference."

"I know," Midge agreed. She thought it was very perceptive of Janet to realize her maturity, even if some other people didn't.

"Aren't you thrilled to death over the prospect of being a bridesmaid?" Janet queried.

"Oh, yes," Midge breathed. And then she asked, her tone a shade anxious, "You don't mind that Tobey didn't ask you to be one of her attendants, do you, Janet?"

"Of course not," her sister said. "Why, at first we weren't even sure Jim could get away so we could come to the wedding."

Midge nodded, and went on confidentially, "I guess Tobey'd have had to ask Alicia to be in it, if she weren't pregnant, or she'd have had her feelings hurt. You know how Alicia is. Then I might have got left out, because Tobey was really awfully anxious to have Suz and Barb. But as things are, everything worked out fine. Weddings," Midge said and wagged her head solemnly, "are terribly complicated to plan."

Janet smiled. "How true! But such fun, aren't they?"

"Gee, yes," Midge concurred wholeheartedly.

The following morning Midge washed her hair again. With a scarf tied around her head to hide the pin curls she went over to Judy's house. She and Judy lay in sling chairs in the Allens' patio, drinking lemonade and eating potato chips and talking for hours. Neither of them could imagine where the time had gone when Midge happened to glance at her wrist watch and realized it was after eleven o'clock.

"I've got to go!" she exclaimed, jumping up. "Tobey was going with Brose to meet his best man's train and Mom will think I'm trying to get out of helping with things."

"Well, aren't you?" Judy laughed.

And Midge had to admit ruefully, "I guess I am, sort of. But I'd better not overdo it."

"When will you get to meet this best man—Johnnie Randall, is it?" Judy's tone was wistful. "He sounds like absolutely the most!"

"Doesn't he?" Midge agreed dreamily. "Of course, Brose could have been kidding me, but I don't think so. I won't get to meet him till tonight, though, at the Gilmans' dinner party."

"Lucky," Judy sighed. "If we weren't such good friends, I'd hate you for having so much fun I can't get in on!"

Midge walked the two blocks home in a happy daydream. Then, just as she turned the corner and came in sight of the big old white house where she had lived all her life, Brose's car drew up before it. And there was the best-looking man she had ever seen in her whole life getting out and helping Tobey down, as Brose slid from beneath the wheel and came around to join them.

Hastily Midge ducked behind a lilac bush, aghast at the sudden realization of pin curls and scarf, old blue jean shorts and crumpled blouse. Besides, she reflected in horror, she'd probably eaten and drunk off all her lipstick. She just couldn't go on and meet the fabulous Johnnie Randall looking like this!

And he really was fabulous, she saw, making a careful check through the sheltering leaves of the lilac bush. Black hair and quizzically narrowed dark eyes, a smile that showed white, white teeth in a deeply tanned face. Broad-shouldered and narrow-hipped and tall—why, Midge thought, her eyes widening in stunned appreciation, he must be six feet three or four at the very least! He was undoubtedly the tallest man she had ever seen, built on such a towering scale that he could make any girl—even one as tall as she—seem little and fragile by comparison. Midge sighed blissfully.

"Aunt Midge—" she jumped at the sound of Stevie's shrill voice behind her—"why you hiding?"

"Shhh," Midge hissed, whirling and grabbing him. "It's a game." She was desperate and that was the first excuse that entered her head.

It seemed to be a good one, because Stevie edged even closer and whispered, his whole face brightening, "Hide-n-seek?"

Midge nodded, then asked, her lips almost touching the little boy's ear as she crouched beside him, "Where's Jimmy?"

"Over at a boy's—that way," Stevie whispered back, pointing. His tone grew indignant, "They wouldn't let me play space men with them 'cause I'm too little."

"Then we'll hide from them, too," Midge murmured, hugging him. Thank goodness, she'd only have one small nephew to cope with!

She peered fearfully through the lilac leaves. Tobey and Brose and Johnnie still stood there, talking. As Midge watched, they started moving toward the house and she breathed a bit easier.

Stevie tugged at her hand. "If Jimmy and that guy don't know we're hiding," he asked reasonably, "why will they look?"

"Oh?" Midge answered absently. "Maybe they won't, Stevie. Maybe it isn't such a good game, after all."

She loosened her restraining hold on her nephew and straightened up to peer once more toward the house. The front door was just closing behind Brose; Tobey and Johnnie had disappeared inside. A moment later Midge could hear the blurred sound of voices, the new arrivals' and those of Janet and Jim and her mother, as Tobey presented Johnnie Randall to them all. They must, Midge realized, be out on the side porch for their voices to come through to her this clearly. And if that was the case, she could sneak in the back door and upstairs to her room without being noticed at all. And in—well, ten minutes at most, she could have changed clothes, brushed out her hair, put on some lipstick—

"What," Stevie asked disappointedly, "we going to do now?"

Midge thought fast. "I have a great idea," she told him. "Let's go home and go in the back way very quietly, so Jimmy won't hear us, even if he happens to be around somewhere quite near. Then I'll get you a nice cold Coke out of the refrig and you can drink it. Okay?"

"Okay." Stevie nodded delightedly.

They hurried across the Heydon lawn toward the back

door, with Midge being careful to keep well out of sight of the porch by guiding Stevie around the opposite side of the house. She went up the back steps on tiptoe, her finger to her lips, and Stevie, his blue eyes glinting, followed suit. In the kitchen, Midge got him his drink as quietly as possible, opened the bottle for him and suggested in a whisper, "Why don't you take it out on the porch? That's where everyone is."

"You coming, too?"

"In a little while," Midge promised, aiming him in the right direction. "Go ahead now."

The noise of his arrival should cover any sound she might make, sneaking through the hall and up the stairs, she felt sure. In a matter of minutes, Midge gained the sanctuary of her own room and closed the door behind her, breathing hard. Of course, a drink right before lunchtime might spoil Stevie's appetite. But this seemed of small moment under the circumstances. Things could have turned out so much more disastrously. Now, then! Midge thought, pulling off her scarf and starting to take out bobby pins with eager fingers.

She worked fast and in practically no time at all stood poised before her mirror for a final appraisal. Her aqua sun dress looked crisply cool and showed off her tan to the most flattering advantage. Her hair lay in soft, if slightly damp, curls high on her neck, where she had tied it back with a white ribbon. Thank goodness her white pumps were clean! She had only to slip into them and—

The sound of voices in the lower hall, obviously saying good-byes, fell like the knell of doom on Midge's ears. Then the front door opened and closed and footsteps receded down the walk. She flew out into the hall and down the stairway just in time to hear Brose and Johnnie Randall slam the car doors and drive away.

"Why—Midge!" Tobey exclaimed in surprise as she turned away from the doorway. "I didn't realize you were home yet." Her eyes widened then as she took in all the details of Midge's impeccable appearance. "Or—are you just going somewhere?"

Midge said, swallowing her disappointment, "No—no, I'm not going anywhere. I was over at Judy's for a while. And then I—I just thought I'd get cleaned up a little."

Mom murmured, "Too bad you didn't realize Brose had brought his friend in so we could all meet him. Such a nice young man! Lovely manners."

"And that Southern drawl." Janet sighed. "Wow!"

"Oh, well." Midge managed a philosophical little shrug, although she was afraid her voice sounded rather quavery. "I'll get to meet him tonight at the Gilmans' dinner."

Honestly, she thought disgustedly, some days it just didn't pay to get up!

# 5

## JOHNNIE

MIDGE had never lived through a longer day, despite the fact that there was something going on practically every minute. But when Judy called up around four o'clock, it seemed to Midge that their morning's talk was far in the past. She had so much to tell Judy that they talked for forty-five minutes straight and only her father's arrival from work made her realize that she had but a little over an hour to get ready for her anticipated meeting with Johnnie Randall. The thought sent delighted little shivers chasing each other up and down her spine.

"I've got to go!" she informed Judy. "I had no idea it was so late! Why didn't you warn me?"

"I didn't know, either," her friend said. "What time is your dinner party?"

"Not till seven," Midge admitted. "But it's at that new restaurant out near Riverdale—you know, The Rendezvous? So we'll be leaving around six-thirty and I have to tear! 'Bye now."

" 'Bye," Judy said. "But remember everything!"

"I will," Midge promised, hanging up.

Never had she bathed and dressed with greater care. She did her nails over twice before they suited her and tried her hair half a dozen different ways until she was finally convinced that her customary pony-tail, with the little circlet of shell flowers holding it in place, really did the most for her after all. She and Judy had decided that she should wear her white polished cotton with the blue polka dots and the matching blue cummerbund that made her waist seem so tiny. Midge donned her white pumps, feeling a pang of regret that Mom hadn't been willing to let her buy some with even higher heels.

She took a last long, appraising look at herself in the mirror, then went into Tobey's room to ask anxiously, "How am I?"

Her sister turned from applying lipstick to smile at Midge approvingly, "Very nice. I love that dress on you."

"It doesn't look awfully young, does it?" Midge asked dubiously.

"Of course not." Tobey shook her head. "It doesn't look any younger than this." She indicated her own soft blue dress with its full skirt and scooped neckline. "Why do you want to look old, for Pete's sake?"

"Not old," Midge admitted, grinning. "Just older, shall we say?" She asked then, turning around, "Are my seams straight?"

Tobey eyed her stockings critically, then nodded. "Perfectly." She turned back to the mirror to smooth her lipstick.

Midge coaxed, peering at the array of bottles on her sister's dresser, "May I use some of your perfume? Mine's all so floral."

"Sure, help yourself," Tobey told her.

Midge proceeded to sniff stoppers thoughtfully until she found the one that seemed just right. As she started to touch the tips of her ears with the enticing scent, Toby warned gently, "Just don't overdo it. A little perfume is intriguing, too much is—" she wrinkled her nose ruefully—"too much!"

"I know." Midge nodded. She asked then, offering the bottle, "You want some of this, too?"

But Tobey reached for a different variety. "This is Brose's favorite and I love to humor the guy. Plain old lily-of-the-valley, wouldn't you know?" She laughed.

Dad's voice, touched with a note of plaintive impatience, reached them from the downstairs hall. "Hey, you two up there! Everyone else is ready and we should be getting started."

"Right away," Tobey called back.

She caught up her little white purse and gloves and she and Midge went down the stairs together.

There were seventeen people at the Gilmans' dinner party. Stevie and Jimmy had been left at home in the capable charge of a neighbor, but all the rest of the Heydon family was there, as were Brose's grandparents from out of town and as many of the wedding party as were available. Since neither Suz nor Barb had arrived yet, there was a wonderful shortage of girls—wonderful, at least, in Midge's estimation. To balance Johnnie Randall and the two ushers, Sox Trevor and George Stearns, there was only Ellen Schultz, who would sing at the wedding, and Midge.

It would be just her luck, Midge thought fleetingly as the party was assembling in the pleasant private dining room overlooking the river, to get stuck between George and Sox at the table. Both of them always treated her as though she were an infant. But, no, she discovered incredulously, her place card was next to Johnnie's, with Sox on her left and Ellen beyond him. Oh, frabjous! Midge thought, her heart swelling with delight.

There had been such a scramble of introductions that she had had no chance to say more than "How do you do" to Johnnie when they met. But she didn't think she had imagined a sort of interested gleam in his dark eyes. And certainly she had never been so moved before by a man's voice merely drawling, "Nice to meet you."

There was an old-world courtliness in the way Johnnie drew out Midge's chair and slid it gently beneath her. Then, as he sat down their hands accidentally brushed, and she felt herself melting like butter. She was afraid the quick color she hated was rising to her cheeks, but maybe, in the candlelight, Johnnie wouldn't notice.

He had the softest, slowest, most beguiling voice, a very personal way of speaking, and a complete inability to sound a final letter R. He murmured, leaning confidentially close to Midge, "The fates ah kind. I was hopin' they'd put me next to you."

So was I, Midge thought, but it didn't seem quite the thing to answer. So she said merely, "Oh?" in a sort of inviting way, as she imagined a woman of the world, accustomed to such compliments, might say it.

Johnnie nodded. His glance was warm, admiring on Midge's face as he remarked, "That Gilman! I'll have to speak to him sevehly."

"Brose?" Midge murmured in surprise. "Why?"

"Livin' with me foh yeahs and neveh once lettin' on that Tobey had a beautiful youngeh sisteh, just leavin' me to find out foh myself."

"Well," Midge managed to answer with a good deal more poise and confidence than she felt, "you can't blame him, really. He was too taken up with Tobey to notice me."

"No man has a right to be so blind," Johnnie insisted. He smiled then. "But I guess I'll fohgive him, as long as we finally got togetheh. Now tell me," he urged, "who all these people ah and how they'eh related to each otheh. I'm confused!"

It was an utterly wonderful evening, one Midge was sure she'd never forget. Johnnie was flatteringly attentive all through dinner and the brief speeches and toasts and good-natured foolery that followed. Midge scarcely heard the speeches, although she laughed at the jokes when the others did. But every word Johnnie said to her was etched indelibly on her memory and not merely for the purpose of relating it all for Judy's benefit later on. Never, Midge thought over and over again, had she met anyone half so attractive and terrific.

The evening held one rather bad moment for her. That was when Ellen Schultz, apparently piqued by Johnnie's indifference, asked with mock casualness, "How's school, Midge? Everything still the same around there?"

Midge could only nod miserably. Now why, she wondered, should Ellen get so catty over Johnnie's attention to her? After all, both Sox and George had been hanging on Ellen's slightest word all through the party. Of course, the two of them put together weren't as entrancing as Johnnie, but Ellen shouldn't covet all the men in sight!

"What college do you go to?" Johnnie asked.

Before Midge could open her lips to answer, Brose spoke to Johnnie from across the table and they became involved in a lively discussion that fortunately pushed his query to Midge entirely out of Johnnie's mind. She felt abjectly grateful to Brose for his accidental intervention. To be taken for a college girl was the most absolutely flattering thing that had ever happened to her. It would have been dreadful to have to disillusion Johnnie. . . .

The next day, rehashing it all for Judy's breathless benefit, Midge admitted, "Honestly, I've never met anyone like him. I mean—well, he's sort of unreal. It's as if a movie actor stepped right off the screen and began saying exciting things to you, looking at you the way girls in movies get looked at."

"Wowie!" Judy sighed, going limp all over in her sling chair and closing her eyes with a beatific expression. "It makes my toes absolutely curl up just to hear about it! I don't see how you can stand it, being right there with him, Midge. How can you think of things to say or anything?"

"I can't always," Midge admitted dreamily. "But with him it doesn't seem to matter. I mean, he says something and then—well, he just looks at you, as if—as if your eyes were answering him and it wasn't really necessary to put things into words."

Judy moaned, "If I met anyone like that, I'd simply die!"

Midge sighed deeply. "And when I think of tonight," she admitted, "I get all shivery. Because Alicia's and Adam's party will be at the country club and, of course, there's the orchestra for dinner dancing." Her voice trailed off. The thought of actually moving around a dance floor in Johnnie Randall's arms was almost more than she could bear. And yet the reality—she checked by her wrist watch—was only a little more than six hours away. Excitement bubbled up in her as she got to her feet.

"I really have to go now," she told her friend. "I'm a fugitive from a lot of work at home, which I promised to do later. But I just had to dash over long enough to tell you about last night."

Judy nodded. "Tonight should be even better—with dancing," she said. "Remember to remember every single thing!"

On Midge's way home, she ran into Bob Pierson. In faded jeans, his back bare and glistening with sweat, he was clipping the Nordquists' hedge.

"Hi," he greeted, waving his big shears. "You're just the one I want to see."

"Why?" Midge asked.

"Are you so tied up with that darned wedding—" Bob grinned ingratiatingly—"that you couldn't go to the movies tonight? There's a western."

Midge said pityingly, "There isn't any movie that could tempt me tonight. Thanks just the same."

"Why?" Bob demanded. "What you doing tonight?"

When Midge explained about the dinner party, he asked plaintively, "Well, gee, couldn't we make the second show? After all, these parties mustn't be much fun for you with a bunch of older people."

Midge laughed mysteriously. "They're not all so old."

"Don't give me that," Bob said. "Name me one who's under twenty."

"Oh, no one's under *that*," Midge admitted, her tone indicating clearly that people under twenty were really pretty juvenile.

Bob frowned at her. "You mean some guy over twenty's giving you a tumble?" Midge found the note of incredulity in his voice pretty insulting.

She shrugged. "I didn't say anything one way or the other. You're the one who's doing all the yacking."

"Well, but, gee—" Bob said.

"Let's just not discuss it any further, okay?" Midge suggested sweetly. "Why don't you ask Judy to the movies? She might go."

"If I'd wanted to take Judy I'd have asked her in the first place," Bob informed her. "Is this guy you're going to see tonight somebody from around here, or who?"

"There are several young men who are going to be ushers and best man and all at the wedding," Midge said airily. "George Stearns and Sox Trevor and Brose's roommate from college."

"George and Sox know how young you are," Bob said flatly. "They wouldn't waste their time. It must be the roommate."

Midge felt her face grow warm and Bob exclaimed

triumphantly, "Yeah, he's the one all right. You're blushing."

"I'm not!" Midge denied furiously. "And anyway, it isn't any of your business, Bob Pierson! You just quit stalling around on that job you're getting paid for and leave my affairs to me!"

She swept past him, her chin in the air, and didn't even turn her head when he called after her, "Gee, Midge, I'm sorry. I didn't mean—"

She would have held her hands over her ears, except that the gesture would have seemed too utterly childish. Much better to simply walk on, coolly and calmly, ignoring him as though he weren't there at all. . . .

The party that night at the country club was even more wonderful than the Gilmans' dinner had been. It was larger by a couple of guests. Tobey's college friend, Suz, and her nice new husband, Denny Bishop, had arrived that afternoon. Midge liked them both on sight. And they didn't disturb the male-female ratio of the group a bit, for which she was grateful.

She didn't get to sit beside Johnnie at the table—trust Alicia to stick her between George and Sox, who talked across her most of the meal. But afterwards, she was the first one Johnnie asked to dance. Midge felt thrilled right down to her toes as he guided her skillfully about the floor, his cheek just brushing her hair, his slow voice saying flattering and amusing and exciting things for her ears alone.

When the dance was over he murmured, "I'll see you lateh. Have to take caeh of a couple of duty dances, but save the one afteh that foh me, will you?"

Midge could only nod, her eyes like stars, her heart racing. She didn't even mind George and Sox being such oafs that neither of them thought of asking her to dance. While Johnnie danced with Ellen, Midge sat and talked with the group around the long, flower-decked table. When he rose to dance with Tobey, Brose suggested, "Shall we give it a whirl, future sister?"

"Okay." Midge smiled. She was really very fond of Brose, who treated her much more like a human being than did most of Tobey's contemporaries.

As they moved around the floor, Brose said, "Johnnie's quite a guy."

"He's nice," Midge agreed. What an understatement!

"His line is absolutely irresistible, I hear." Brose chuckled. "Had half the girls at college mooning over him. Even those he had no intention of making a play for were always getting in his hair. I guess that Texas charm, combined with his looks and money, is pretty potent."

Midge merely nodded. She felt like saying, "But if you're trying to warn me, just don't bother." Still, she was sure Brose meant well, so there seemed no point in getting mad.

One man, she reflected, was never capable of understanding another the way a woman could. A man saw only the surface, not what was deep down underneath.

"The Casanova type," Brose mused, "with the added attraction of a southern accent—that's old Johnnie."

Midge didn't agree. She didn't agree at all. The thing was, Brose just didn't understand. . . .

# 6

## A LESSON FOR MIDGE

BARB WALTERS arrived Thursday morning, a strikingly pretty girl, with dark hair and pixy features, whose charm seemed enhanced by the bright-framed glasses she almost always wore. She had acquired a golden tan since her family's move to Florida and her quick wit and gay smile were even more enchanting than Midge had remembered. Tobey took her up to her room to unpack and Midge could hear them talking and laughing in there, catching up on all the exciting things that had happened to each of them during their separation.

Busy as Midge was, she felt a little left out and lonely after Barb came. Mom was occupied with the caterer, getting ready for the buffet supper that would follow the wedding rehearsal that evening. Janet and Suz were trying to shift things about in the library, so as to make room for more wedding presents, utilizing their willing husbands' strength to move the heavier furniture. They were having a lot of fun, talking and joking as they worked. But they were all so married, Midge felt like a fifth wheel in their company. She was delighted when Judy dropped in late in the morning, ostensibly to see the newest gifts, but actually Midge knew, to hear a full report on the party the night before.

At first she and Judy had no chance for private talk. The library teemed with people, the caterer's crew overran the kitchen and dining room, Jimmy and Stevie were playing Slap with an old deck of cards on the porch and Mom had declared the living room off limits lest its pristine order and cleanliness be disturbed. Midge considered taking Judy up to her bedroom, but changed her mind when Tobey and Barb came downstairs. There was too much going on that she didn't want to miss.

Then the problem resolved itself, but in a way Midge didn't like at all! Tobey and Barb decided to drive over to the Gilmans', so that the maid of honor and the best man could meet and have a little chance to get acquainted before the rehearsal that night. There was nothing Midge could do, despite the sinking sensation in her tummy. It would have sounded queer had she objected to the plan, although every instinct in her opposed it. Tobey and Brose, Barb and Johnnie—why, it sounded like a regular foursome!

Midge hoped the abject misery she was feeling didn't show in her face, as Tobey and Barb went out to the car. She spoke glumly to Judy. "Let's go up to my room where we can talk."

Somehow a lot of the dazzle had gone out of her memories of the night before, although Judy listened with eager interest to everything Midge had to tell her.

Finally Judy exclaimed, flopping over on her back on Midge's bed and staring with wide shining eyes at the ceiling, "I think it's the most absolutely terrific thing

I ever heard! An older man like that! Didn't you just practically die, dancing with him?"

Midge nodded moodily. "Just practically."

"And then going out on the terrace in the moonlight—" Judy broke off with an ecstatic little sigh. She asked then, hesitantly, "Did he—well, put his arm around you or—or try to kiss you?"

"Of course not," Midge denied. "He was simply showing me the stars. He knows absolutely everything about astronomy."

"I'll bet," Judy agreed enviously.

"Once," Midge admitted, "he did put his hand on my shoulder, but that was just to turn me around so I'd see where the Big Dipper was. I was looking the wrong direction."

"I would have, too." Judy giggled. When Midge didn't join in her mirth, she sat up suddenly and stared at her, frowning. "I must say you don't sound very elated about it all. You're not tired of him already, are you?"

"Oh, no!" Midge exclaimed feelingly. Who could ever grow tired of Johnnie? She went on, moved by a strong urge to confide her misgivings to someone and sure that she could trust Judy not to give her secret away, "The thing is, now that Barb's here, I'm scared he'll get interested in her. She's so cute—and so much older."

Judy's frown deepened sympathetically. "Yeah, she is that, all right. Gee, Midge, you don't really suppose he'll—"

But Midge didn't let her finish. She couldn't bear

to hear the ugly possibility put into words again. It had been hard enough to mention it herself. She broke in, trying to keep her tone light, "Oh, he may not go for her type at all. He certainly hasn't paid much attention to Ellen and look how attractive she is."

Judy nodded. "That's right." She sounded a bit more cheerful.

"Anyway," Midge's shrug was the height of assumed casualness, "we'll just have to wait and see how he reacts tonight, when Barb and I are both around. That'll tell the story."

Just then the noonday whistle sounded from the shoe factory over on the other side of town and Judy leaped up, exclaiming, "Golly, I've got to tear! My mother'll have a kitten! But I'll be dying to know what happens. Let me know first thing in the morning, will you?"

"Sure," Midge agreed. She even managed a smile, although it hurt her face a little.

"Wedding rehearsals," announced the balding young minister, Dr. Beecher, "are always a mess, so don't be disturbed because things aren't going very smoothly. And believe me, I speak from years of experience." He chuckled. "Why, if a rehearsal ever went off like clockwork, I'd be worried."

The group of a dozen or so people, assembled in the two front pews of the church, smiled in response to his smile, but they looked rather doubtful just the same.

And Brose asked plaintively, "Are they always this big a mess, though? If we don't get things straightened out a little, I'm afraid I'll end up married to the wrong girl."

The laughter that followed his remark rather hollowly must have served to loosen the tension a bit. Because the next run-through of the external details of the ceremony went off almost without a hitch.

"We'll let well enough alone now." The minister beamed at them all, one hand on Tobey's shoulder and the other on Brose's. "I'm sure everyone understands his part in the proceedings. You'll see, it will go perfectly tomorrow night."

"I hope so," Tobey said softly, her eyes lifting to Brose's.

His arm went around her, his look said he loved her as clearly as though he had put it into words for all to hear.

Johnnie Randall spoke feelingly, "I'm not goin' to lose that ring if I have to pin it onto me with a safety pin."

Barb laughed up at him. "You should patent that brilliant idea, Johnnie. It could start a fad among best men."

Midge's heart twisted miserably to see them.

Because Johnnie was looking at Barb just as he had looked at her, Midge, last night and the night before. His dark eyes glowed between their narrowed lids with unmistakable liking and interest. His mouth curved in an agreeable grin and his hand, even as Midge looked on, reached out to cup Barb's elbow and squeeze it.

"I just might do that." He chuckled.

As if, Midge thought unhappily, I weren't here at all!

And she wished that she weren't, but there was no escape. Both at the church and afterward at the buffet supper at home, she could do nothing but stay and watch, while the thing between Barb and Johnnie grew and solidified before her eyes. It would have seemed strange had Midge crept away from all the laughter and gaiety, the relatives and friends milling about. But that was what she wished she could do. Even the table, festively decorative and piled high with wonderful food, scarcely tempted her. She ate half a dozen tiny sandwiches and a little shrimp salad and a piece of light cake and chocolate cake, just so no one would notice her lack of appetite and ask if she were ill, thus drawing attention to her misery. But her heart wasn't in it.

How could a man be so fickle, she asked herself again and again before the endless evening was over. Even a man such as Brose had said Johnnie was, a Casanova with a southern accent. The fascinated way he had looked at her, the tone of his voice—and now going through the same routine with Barb. He even acted, Midge thought miserably, as though he was enjoying himself a little more with Barb. Or did it just seem that way because she was now on the outside, looking in?

Even when the party and its aftermath of sleepy talk was finally over, it seemed as though the image of Barb and Johnnie, having such a wonderful time together, remained etched against Midge's eyelids as she closed them and tried to go to sleep. The thing that hurt most was that Johnnie had been just as friendly and gay with her, as he was with all the others. His attitude had set her to wondering whether she could have imagined his earlier personal interest; or had he just been friendly then, too?

She turned over and over in bed, bunched her pillow, smoothed it out again, pulled the sheet over her, then kicked it off. Still sleep eluded her. From Tobey's room across the hall, she could hear the muted sound of her sister and Barb, talking and talking and talking.

Tobey shouldn't stay awake so late, Midge thought virtuously—or was it jealously? Barb should let her get to sleep. The bride shouldn't have circles under her eyes. But neither should the bridesmaid, Midge told herself sternly. And she wasn't sleeping, either. *Johnnie, Johnnie,* a sad little voice called out from somewhere deep within her. *How could you do this to me? How could you be so mean?*

After a while Midge heard her door open quietly and then Tobey's voice, only a breath above a whisper, asked, "Midge, you asleep?"

"Huh-uh," Midge whispered back.

Her eyes, accustomed to the darkness, could just make out her sister's white-pajamaed figure as she crossed to sit down on the edge of the bed.

Tobey said, "I heard your springs creaking and was afraid we were keeping you awake."

"It wasn't that," Midge said. "It's okay."

"Midge," Tobey's hand rested momentarily on her shoulder, "is anything the matter? You seemed so quiet tonight—sort of aloof."

Tobey's touch, her sympathetic tone, opened the floodgates. Midge began in an indignant whisper, "It's that Johnnie," and went on to tell Tobey the whole miserable story. Somehow, even as she talked, she found herself feeling better. The things that had ached so, bottled up inside her, lost some of their power to hurt when she confided them to her sister. She finished ruefully, "The thing that gets me is that I'm not sure now whether he meant anything at all, or if I just imagined it. What do you think?"

"You didn't imagine it," Tobey told her. "He did pay a lot of attention to you. But the thing you've got to learn is that sweet-talking someone just comes natural to men like Johnnie. They can't help it, I guess, any more than they can stop breathing. You happened to appeal to him more than any other unattached female around, even if you were a bit young. So he concentrated on you for a while. Then Barb turned up, so now she's the one. On the plane going back to Texas, he'll probably be real attentive to his seat-mate, if she's fairly attractive. Or one of the stewardesses."

"You mean—" Midge asked doubtfully—"you don't think his interest in Barb means anything—any more than it did when he acted interested in me?"

"No, I don't," Tobey said. "And I don't think Barb's does, either. In fact, Barb's a little bit that way herself. Her interest in Johnnie doesn't mean much, either. It's just a sort of reflex action when she meets an attractive man."

"Yeah?" Midge murmured wonderingly.

"The thing is," Tobey said, getting to her feet and pulling the sheet up over Midge, "girls just have to learn to take the Johnnies of this world in their stride. They're very charming, very attractive, but they just go through the motions of making love as they'd play tennis or golf or any other game they happen to enjoy and be good at."

"But, don't they ever really fall in love?"

"Oh, sure," Tobey said. "And they usually fall hard, too. But, personally, I'd prefer a man who wasn't quite so adept at it all that I couldn't help suspecting he'd had a good deal of practice. Someone like Brose," she finished softly. "The faithful type."

Thinking of Brose made Midge exclaim, "You should be asleep, Tobey! After all, tomorrow—"

"I know," Tobey whispered on her way to the door. "Tomorrow's the day! And you know what I hope?"

"What?" Midge asked.

"I hope that sometime you'll be as happy as I am right this minute." The door closed quietly behind her.

Lying there in the still darkness, Midge felt a little smile tug at her lips. Tobey was sweet. But then, the thought of Johnnie's dark, smiling face intruded on her thoughts and her own smile faded. A little of the hurt crept back to ache heavily within her. Not so sharp as before, but not gone yet.

Midge lay quietly for a while, her eyes shut, trying to sleep. But then a memory caught at her and she got up, being careful not to let the springs squeak under her shifting weight. She padded across the familiar room silently, opened the closet door and stood on tiptoe to rummage around on the top shelf. Then she went back to bed and curled up once more, but this time she wasn't alone. On the pillow beside her, his ancient fur a bit rough against her arm, lay her toy dog, Pootsie, just as he had lain so many times before.

Good old Pootsie, Midge thought, as drowsiness crept deliciously through her. He was still quite a comforter. . . .

# ]

## THE SEARCH

IT RAINED during the night and the skies were
still gray and overcast when Midge wakened.
"Oh, no!" she whispered aloud, sitting straight up
in bed to look out the window.

A wet-leaved branch of maple met her appalled eye
and, beyond it, soggy green lawn and rain-washed street.
Such weather on Tobey's wedding day? It just couldn't
be! But it was.

Midge swung her feet over the side of the bed and
something hit the floor with a soft thump. She glanced
down, frowning in faint bewilderment to see shabby
old Pootsie lying there on the scatter rug. Then memory
washed over her in a hurting tide.

*Johnnie,* she thought desolately. *Johnnie and Barb.*
*Johnnie and anybody but me.*

She might as well get used to the idea, though. Face
up to it until it lost the power to make her throat ache
and her eyelids sting. As Tobey had said last night, a
girl just had to learn to take the Johnnies of this world
in stride. Well, she'd had her first hard lesson, taken
the first wobbly step. Maybe the rest would come more
easily for her. She hoped so.

The thing to do, she told herself firmly, was to simply

put all thought of Johnnie out of her mind. Concentrate on other things. Keep busy. This shouldn't be hard, Midge reflected with a wry little smile. Not today, of all days.

Already, from down in the kitchen, she could hear faint sounds of people moving about, muffled voices and laughter, the subdued clatter of dishes. Midge glanced at her dresser clock and saw with surprise that it was almost nine. Mom and Dad were undoubtedly up, as were Stevie and Jimmy and probably their parents. Maybe Suz and Denny were downstairs by this time, too.

She dressed quickly and quietly in yellow skirt and a sleeveless white blouse, tied back her hair, slipped her bare feet into white ballerinas. Down in the kitchen, she was engulfed in a crowd. As she had suspected, everyone was up except Barb and Tobey. Mom and Janet were just getting breakfast on the table, crisp bacon and eggs, sweet rolls warm from the oven, fruit juice and coffee. It smelled so good, Midge felt quite starved. Everyone was talking about the weather and hoping it would clear before evening. There was an undercurrent of excitement, of anticipation, making the very atmosphere crackle.

They were almost finished with breakfast, just lingering over coffee, when Tobey and Barb came downstairs.

"What a day!" Tobey exclaimed. "We just haven't been living right, I guess."

But she looked so perfectly radiant and happy, you

could tell that the weather really made very little difference to her.

"It just has to clear up!" Barb said. "Now if only you lived in Florida—"

"Or California," Jim put in drily.

But Dad admonished, "None of that Chamber of Commerce stuff now. There's nothing wrong with the climate in the middle west. And anyway, the radio weather broadcast said, 'Clearing and cooler.' So what's wrong with that?"

"You don't call off weddings on account of rain, like baseball games, do you?" Jimmy asked anxiously.

Over the laughter that followed, Tobey's amused voice assured him, "Definitely not! This wedding's coming off if we all have to row to church."

"In boats?" Stevie asked hopefully.

"It's a joke, son." Big Jim chuckled. "Don't get your hopes up."

Going along with her intention to keep busy every minute, Midge helped Janet and Suz with the dishes. Usually this was a job she hated, but not today. There was so much to talk about, to laugh over. Midge found she liked Tobey's college friend better, the more contact she had with her. Suz seemed rather plain and quiet until you got to know her well enough to appreciate her complete naturalness and friendly warmth. No wonder, Midge thought, Tobey was so fond of her.

All their talk was of the wedding, of the day ahead. The big reception would be held in the church parlors after the ceremony, with members of the Women's Society preparing and serving the food. Later, just a few close friends and the two families would gather at the Heydons'. Still, there had been a lot of details for Mom to take care of. And the way the phone kept ringing every few minutes, it seemed these hadn't all been settled yet.

Suz said feelingly to Janet, "I hope my children will be boys, like yours, so I'll never have to go through this."

Barb was upstairs with Tobey, helping her pack, and Mom was on the phone talking to the florist and Dad had been sent out on some urgent errand when the doorbell rang. Midge went to answer it and there were the two ushers, in jeans and tee shirts, their faces wreathed in smiles and their heads full of nefarious plans to locate what Sox called the get-away car and decorate it appropriately.

"Can't let old Brose off too easy," George Stearns said, "or he'd think his pals didn't love him."

"We've got my car trunk full of old shoes, tin cans, JUST MARRIED signs and paint." Sox grinned fiendishly. "Now all we have to do is find the car."

Janet and Suz had come out into the hall behind Midge and now Janet said, "But they're using the Gilmans' car for their honeymoon, not that old one of Brose's."

"We know," George agreed. "And Brose's wreck is right there in the Gilmans' garage, large as life. But the Gilmans' car has completely disappeared. Strange, isn't it?"

Suz looked rather blank, until Midge explained that hiding the bridegroom's car was a time-honored custom in Edgewood. Then his friends tried to locate it and add all the trimmings they deemed so necessary. The poor groom always sought a most unlikely hiding place, usually in the closed garage of some old family friend his contemporaries didn't even know about. But the eager ushers and bridesmaids were almost always successful in ferreting it out, even though it might take them the greater part of the wedding day to do so.

"This is all new to me," Suz said, shaking her head, "but it sounds like fun."

"Oh, it is," Janet agreed, her eyes shining. "And I can still remember what a mess poor Jim's car was when we got married. So why should Tobey and Brose escape unscathed?"

Denny Bishop and Jim, who had been hobnobbing on the side porch, joined the group in the hallway then and entered into the plot with the greatest enthusiasm. It was decided that the two married couples, along with young Jimmy and Stevie, should go in the Bishops' car. Midge would accompany Sox and George and they would stop at the Schultz's house and pick up Ellen. Barb, of course, would stick with Tobey, and since the best man always remained true to his trust, there was no point in getting Johnnie.

"But if the bunch of us can't locate that car," Sox said in a do-or-die tone, "we're not as smart as I think."

There began such a chase, such a combing of the Gilmans' neighbors' garages, such questionings and deductions, as should have unearthed half a dozen hidden cars instead of just one. And yet that one remained mysteriously missing, tantalizingly out of reach.

"It can't just disappear," Midge exclaimed. "It's too big."

"I think we should broaden our base of operations," Sox suggested like a general plotting a military maneuver. "Old Brose is too bright to hide it right in his own neighborhood. Whom do the Gilmans know in other parts of town?"

He pulled over to the curb and stopped the car. The one driven by Denny Bishop drew up behind them and everybody spilled out for a full-scale conference. Only it developed that the second car load was chickening out.

"Do you nuts realize it's afternoon?" Janet demanded. "I've got to get the kids home for lunch."

So that was why she was feeling so hollow, Midge realized. She was practically starving. Not a bite to eat since breakfast.

Suz said regretfully, "I'm afraid we're on a wild-goose chase. Brose has his car too well hidden."

Jim and Denny seemed to share their wives' opinions.

But George objected, "Give up and go home before we find it and decorate it? Never!"

Sox nodded vigorously and Midge and Ellen agreed. "Only can't we get something to eat and then go on?" Midge asked.

"Sure, we'll treat you to a hamburger," George offered magnanimously.

"Ah, to be young and full of spizzerinctum." Jim grinned. "Good luck to all you earnest searchers. We'll see you later."

After a bite to eat at Joe's Grill, Midge and Ellen, Sox and George, continued doggedly with their hunt.

They explored several possibilities they'd dreamed up over lunch, but to no avail.

"Let's stop by at the Gilmans'," George suggested. "Maybe we can twist Johnnie's arm and make him spill something."

Midge's heart gave a miserable sort of flop at the mention of Johnnie's name. Still, when she realized how long it had been since she'd thought of him, she felt better.

Even talking to him face to face didn't hurt as much as she had expected. Brose and Johnnie came out in response to Sox's summoning honk and just lounged there on the edge of the drive, taunting them good-humoredly.

"Why don't you jokers give up and go home?" Brose chortled. "Don't you know when you're licked?"

"We've hardly even started looking," George answered, but he didn't sound as confident as he had earlier.

"That cah's in good company," Johnnie drawled. "You all ah wastin' youah time huntin'."

They lingered for a while longer, ribbing each other, hoping against hope the groom or the best man might drop some accidental hint that would prove useful. But none was forthcoming.

Driving around once more, Ellen was the first to show signs of weakening. "We can't just spend the whole day looking for the darned car," she objected. "I probably won't be able to sing a note as it is, with it being so damp and all."

As though on cue, at her words, the sun broke through

the hovering clouds to bathe them with wonderful brilliance.

"Look at that!" Sox exclaimed. "It's a sign we shouldn't give up yet."

"Of all the ridiculous—" Ellen began disgustedly.

But Midge, who had been sitting quietly, thinking, interrupted. "You know," she said frowning, "I've been trying to figure out what that remark of Johnnie's meant —about the car being in good company?"

"I don't get it," Sox said.

And George shook his head. "Doesn't make sense to me."

But Midge was off in hot pursuit of a vague idea. "Where would a car be in good company, do you suppose?"

George scratched his bristling crew-cut reflectively. "With a lot of other cars?" His tone was questioning.

"You don't suppose the rat would hide it in a public garage!" Sox was beginning to sound excited.

"Or a used-car lot?" George suggested.

"Here we go again," Ellen murmured a shade wearily.

"Party pooper!" Sox accused as he turned the corner and headed the car resolutely back toward the main part of town.

But a check of all the garages and every used car lot in Edgewood failed to turn up the Gilmans' green sedan.

"It was a good thought," Sox told Midge, "even if it didn't work out. At least, you're trying."

"There's one other possibility," Midge said a bit hesitantly, ignoring Ellen's martyred look. "You know that old carriage house of Miss Tess Wentworth's? The

Gilmans know her. And I suppose you could figure a car was in good company with a lot of old surreys and sleighs and—things—wouldn't you?" Her voice sort of ran down under the impact of three very dubious expressions.

But then Sox shrugged. "Oh, well, I guess it's worth a try, if nobody's got any better idea."

So off they drove to Miss Tess' ginger-bready carriage house, with its sagging doors and be-cupola-ed top. "She takes a nap in the afternoon," Midge told the others. "And the carriage house is 'way at the back of her yard. She'll never hear us."

"This is positively the last place—" Ellen began.

But the boys shushed her unfeelingly, drawing up at the curb near the seldom-used graveled drive. Ellen sat stubbornly in the car as Midge and the two boys got out and went over to open one of the heavy doors. Not too hopefully they advanced a few steps into the dusty interior. It was dim and cobwebby. Mouldering harness hung on the walls and there was an old surrey with fringe and a two-wheeled buggy and a sleigh with rusty runners. There was also a vintage car, high and old-fashioned and beyond it—Midge squinted unbelievingly —the Gilmans' familiar sedan, looking strangely out of place in such surroundings. Their search was ended.

George let out a restrained whoop and gestured to Ellen, who came running. Sox whirled to give Midge a bear hug that lifted her off her feet.

"What a brain!" he exclaimed. "What deductive powers! Old Sherlock had nothing on you, kid!"

Midge felt a warm glow of satisfaction as Sox and

George began lugging from the car trunk all the para-phenalia they had been carrying around so hopefully. The hand-lettered signs. The tin cans on wires. The ancient shoes. The paint, which, mercifully, was the kind that could be washed off.

"Don't just stand there," George ordered. "Let's get cooking."

As the four of them fell to with enthusiasm, Midge realized that a part of the deep-down delight she felt was due to the fact that it had been she who read Johnnie's cryptic remark correctly. Maybe that would pay him back just a little for the way he had treated her.

# 8

## THE WEDDING

WEDDINGS, Midge thought, seemed different when you were right in the midst of them, a performer, so to speak, rather than a mere onlooker. The minister's words sounded oddly personal, heard at such close range. And from her vantage point near the bank of white gladioli that framed the altar, Midge could see the way Brose's hand shook as he slipped the ring on Tobey's finger. Nor was Tobey's hand quite steady when she gave Brose his ring. And there were beads of perspiration on Johnnie's forehead and on those of the two ushers, standing so stiffly straight beyond him. But viewed from the pews, neither nerves nor perspiration would be apparent. The soft pastel dresses of the bride's attendants, the stark black and white garb of the groomsmen, would frame effectively the lovely central figure of Tobey, the bride.

Everything had gone off smoothly, despite the confused rehearsal last night. The bridesmaids' tread had been measured and graceful, coming up the aisle. Dad had looked solemnly handsome and Tobey, on his arm, so beautiful in white lace, with short crisp veil falling from beneath a little pearl-embroidered cap, that she seemed almost unreal.

But she looked real enough at close range, Midge reflected with a faint smile. She looked so happy it made your throat hurt and your eyes feel all misty just to see her. And suddenly the ceremony was over and the organ notes swelled out richly and sweetly and Brose was kissing Tobey as though he could scarcely let her go.

Midge found herself remembering the last line of all the fairy tales she had loved so as a child. "And they lived happily ever after." That was the way she hoped it would be for Tobey and Brose.

Even Sox's cynical comment, "Another good man gone wrong," as he gave Midge his arm for their walk back down the aisle couldn't puncture her mood of vicarious romance.

His rather sheepish grin indicated clearly he didn't really mean it. Men always felt they had to be sarcastic at a time like this, Midge supposed. Otherwise how could they maintain that fine masculine disdain for all things sentimental?

"Your turn will come," she whispered back to him.

And Sox looked as though the idea wasn't in the least distasteful.

The rest of the evening moved in an exciting blur for Midge. There were pictures to be taken, the big white cake to be cut with a ribboned knife, punch to be drunk and delicious little sandwiches nibbled at. There were people to talk to, compliments to acknowledge, as everyone milled about in the church parlor.

And then, later, there was the mad ride all around town, in a honking, hilarious parade, made up of the wedding party and several other carloads of Tobey's and

Brose's friends. In the lead was the Gilmans' fantastically decorated car, driven by Johnnie, with Barb on the front seat beside him and the bridal couple in the back. They had been philosophical about the thwarting of their efforts to keep the car hidden. Tobey had laughed ruefully, murmuring, "Anyway, we tried." And Brose had sighed, "I knew it was too much to hope that some of you jokers wouldn't outsmart me. Oh, well, at least a guy only has to go through this once." Now they seemed oblivious of all but each other, untroubled by the flapping JUST MARRIED signs, the clattering of tin cans and the thumping of old shoes. They sat there, confetti dusting their heads and shoulders, hands locked together, lost in a secret world of their own.

Still later, a small nucleus of family and close friends gathered at the Heydons to see the honeymooners off and wish them Godspeed. While Suz and Barb were upstairs helping Tobey get ready to leave, someone put some records on the phonograph and Johnnie asked Midge to dance. Moving around the living room in his arms, with half a dozen others dancing, too, Midge felt a little ache for something lost and sweet that she might never experience again. Because now she knew that she was just a girl to dance with, so far as Johnnie was concerned, just someone to flatter and talk softly to, as he had to so many others and would to so many more.

It doesn't mean a thing, Midge told herself, as her feet followed easily where he led, as his chin brushed her forehead.

She supposed it was grown-up to realize this, to feel aloof, as though she weren't personally involved in the situation. But it had been fun while it lasted, she thought with a wry little smile.

"Why so quiet?" Johnnie murmured, lips close to her ear.

"Just thinking," Midge answered.

"About me, I hope." He said it almost automatically, as though the words were just part of a familiar line, one he used so often he didn't even have to think about it.

She wouldn't have noticed that earlier, Midge realized. She'd have been far too dazzled. But no more. Oh, she was learning.

She was spared the necessity of answering his remark. There was a sound of a door opening and voices in the upstairs hall. Then Tobey and Barb and Suz came down and everyone converged in the hallway. Tobey looked glowing and happy in her pale blue suit and little white hat. She stood on tiptoe on the lower step to toss her bouquet into the waving mass of feminine hands reaching up to receive it. Ellen caught it and Midge felt a small unworthy prick of satisfaction over the fact that it hadn't gone to Barb.

Tobey gave Midge a quick hug, but there was no chance for any really personal word in the burst of good-byes, the tide of good-luck wishes, the embraces and kisses that ended only when Tobey and Brose escaped into the summer night. They hurried out to the Gilmans' car arm in arm and climbed in just as Sox and Johnnie finished stowing away their luggage and slamming down the trunk lid. Johnnie had got rid of the tin cans and old shoes, but the big JUST MARRIED sign and the humorous slogans painted on the car itself remained for all to see.

Brose would stop at the first garage he came to and get the car washed, Midge knew. But anyone who looked into his and Tobey's faces wouldn't need signs to tell that they were newly married. She sighed a small sigh, feeling at once happy and forlorn. Happy for Tobey, forlorn for herself. It was over. Tobey was married. And she, Midge, was the last Heydon daughter left at home.

Even in the midst of the chattering, laughing crowd that drifted back into the living room, Midge felt a sudden chill sense of letdown. She realized that her feet were starting to hurt, from wearing high heels such a long time. And her face felt stiff with smiling.

Dad came up beside her and put an arm around her shoulders. "Well," he said, "I'm glad we've got you left."

And Mom, who always claimed she never cried over weddings, smiled at Midge and nodded in agreement. But it seemed to Midge her eyes were unnaturally bright.

"I'm going to make some coffee," Janet announced. "And they brought over a whole tray of leftover sandwiches from the church and there's loads more cake."

Somehow, Midge's spirits lifted a little at the prospect of more food. And she was grateful for the lingering guests, for all the talk and laughter. Even when the others left, there'd be Suz and Denny and Barb until tomorrow and Janet and Jimmy and the boys for a couple of days after that.

But it would seem queer, Midge faced the realization

squarely, when things got back to normal and there were just Mom and Dad and her. Then a new thought struck her, one that had been sort of pushed aside in all the excitement of the wedding. In just another week, Judy and she and Mom and Dad would be heading for Green Lake and their vacation. And that week, Midge knew, would be so filled with plans and preparations for their departure that there'd be no time left for brooding. Why, she didn't have a thing in the world to worry about! By the time they got back from the lake, she'd have grown accustomed to the idea of getting along without Tobey.

Relievedly, Midge followed Janet out to the kitchen to help her get the coffee ready.

# 9

## MIDGE DOES A FAVOR

M IDGE AND Judy went shopping together Wednesday morning, for shorts and a beach coat for Midge and a new bathing suit for her friend. Since neither of them was prone to buy the first article shown them, these purchases occupied several hours. They stopped in at Joe's Grill for hamburgers and malts on their way home, stacking their bags and boxes high on the table beside them.

"Honestly," Judy said, her dark eyes shining, "I can hardly wait till Saturday. It's going to be so exciting!"

Midge said, "Don't get your hopes too high. It's just a medium-sized lake and certainly our cottage isn't anything to brag about. I mean, it's comfortable enough and close to the beach, but it's pretty old."

"But the swimming," Judy said dreamily, smoothing a lock of her short-cut dark hair back from her forehead, "and the boys."

Midge felt a little uncomfortable. She had tried not to build up Judy's expectations, but Judy seemed to come to a boil even without encouragement. Midge said, "Well—you never can tell for sure about the boys. Some years there's a pretty good selection and others it's strictly from hunger. Now last year, there weren't

81

enough to go around and the ones there were—" she wrinkled her nose expressively. "Of course," she admitted, "I was only fourteen last summer and the ones who hung around me were mere children."

"It'll be different, now we're grown up," Judy said staunchly. "You'll see."

"Optimist." Midge grinned.

"Well, it's bound to be," Judy argued. "After all, your folks have been going there for years. You must know a sort of backlog of boys. And that always helps you get acquainted with any new ones that turn up."

"I read an article the other day," Midge told Judy, "about how there are more women than men in the world and it's getting worse all the time. That's probably why there are always more girls than boys at summer resorts. Maybe," she explored the idea further, "by the time we're old enough to marry we won't be able to find husbands."

"Don't be *silly!*" Judy exclaimed. "I read the article, too. It'll be years before there's a real problem—" she broke off to ask piteously, "won't it?"

"I suppose so," Midge agreed. "But just the same—"

"Hi," a masculine voice interrupted her.

"Speaking of boys, here's one right now," Judy said brightly.

But it was only Bob Pierson, so Midge couldn't get too excited.

After casual greetings had been exchanged, Bob said, "Why don't you shove all those packages over and I'll sit with you."

"Lucky us," Midge drawled.

But Judy shifted the packages and Bob sat down and began asking questions about the wedding. "All your company left?"

Midge nodded. "The house is positively echoing, it's so empty."

"Even," Bob asked, "the fascinating old guy from Texas?" There was a nasty note of sarcasm in his voice.

Before Midge could answer, a waitress brought the soda and sandwich Bob had ordered. And by the time she left, Midge's flash of anger had faded, so that she stated merely, "Everybody's gone." Bob's attitude was so childish, it wasn't worth while to argue.

"In that case," he suggested, "maybe you'll condescend to go to the movies with ordinary people again. How about tonight?"

Judy looked so wistful that Midge suggested, "Get a date for Judy, too, and we'll double. Okay?"

"Okay," Bob agreed, his blue eyes lighting.

When they had finished lunch and were out on the street Bob said, "I'd help you carry all those packages home, but I've got to get back to work. I'm cutting the Mosers' back yard and it's a monster."

"Still saving your money for a car?" Midge queried.

Bob nodded. "And I will be for quite a while. Cars are expensive."

He lifted a hand in salute and said, "I'll round up somebody for Judy and we'll pick you up at seven. Be ready."

"We will," Judy said happily and Bob strode off in the direction of the Mosers.

As the girls turned their steps toward home, Judy said,

her tone grateful, "Thanks for fixing it up for me to-night."

"Wait till you see whom he gets," Midge suggested. "He may round up another creep."

"You consider Bob a creep?" Judy asked, appalled. "I think he's cute. Why are you so mean to him all the time?"

"He's good-looking," she went on, "even if he isn't terribly tall. He's taller than either of us, at least."

"You want him?" Midge suggested generously.

"Don't be silly!" Judy shook her head. "He's absolutely crazy about you. Anyone can see that."

"I can't." Midge shook her head. "He just asks me out because he feels a boy his age should date a girl once in a while and he's used to me, so he doesn't mind. That's how crazy he is about me."

"I don't think you understand Bob," Judy said solemnly.

Actually, their double date was more fun than Midge had anticipated. Bob brought along Pete Holmes for Judy and Pete had a crazy sense of humor that kept everyone laughing. The movie was good, too, and afterward they had sodas at Joe's and ran into several contemporaries. So even with Bob, Midge had a good time. It was sort of funny about Bob, she thought. He was nice looking enough and actually his conversation wasn't dull. It was just that they were so well acquainted, it was like going out with a brother—if she had a brother. She enjoyed herself, but it didn't seem like a real date at all. There was no spark, no sense of excitement, such as her most casual contacts with other boys gave her.

They left Judy and Pete in front of Judy's house and strolled on through the summer night toward the Heydons. There was a moon and it made little lacy patterns through the leaves. And the soft air carried a scent of mock orange. A romantic sort of night, Midge reflected with a faint sigh. Too bad to waste it.

Bob was talking about cars again and Midge had only been listening with half an ear. Then something he said brought her wandering attention back sharply. "If a guy was ever lucky enough to find a *real* old car, what a break that would be!"

"How old?" Midge queried, a vague memory stirring in her.

"Older the better," Bob answered. "The only trouble is, there aren't many of them around any more. Used to be a guy could pick one up for peanuts and fix it all up, get it into first-class shape and really have something. Now most of 'em have been fixed up and they cost a mint, even if their owners were willing to sell, which they usually aren't." He went on regretfully, "All I've got saved up is eighty-five bucks and that wouldn't buy the headlights on a real old bus. My best bet's a third-or-fourth-hand jaloppy and they haven't got any real class. Still, it would be something to fix up and fool around with till I'm old enough to get my license."

Midge had pinned down the vagrant memory that troubled her. She had seen an old car just lately. One that was doing nothing more constructive than gathering dust and cobwebs in Miss Tess' carriage house. A faint smile curved Midge's lips at the thought of what Bob would do for a chance at a car like that. But it wouldn't be fair to mention it and get his hopes up, not till she spoke to Miss Tess and found out if she'd be willing to sell it. Midge couldn't help wondering whether Miss Tess even remembered it was there. . . .

But Miss Tess recalled the old car perfectly, Midge discovered, when she broached the subject to her the next day. Adam Wentworth's aunt sat with Midge in the large ornately furnished drawing room with its gold-framed family pictures and old-fashioned bric-a-brac, its richly brocaded drapes and Oriental rugs. They were having tea. Whenever you called on Miss Tess in the afternoon, you were served tea in thin Haviland cups and tiny frosted cakes on a silver tray. Miss Tess had always had afternoon tea and she always would. Not that Midge minded. The little cakes, baked by Miss Tess' competent housekeeper, were invariably delicious.

Midge was very fond of Miss Tess. She was extremely old and so fragile she looked almost breakable. Blue veins showed through her delicately wrinkled skin and you could see the shape of her bone structure in her forehead beneath the snowy hair. But her eyes were bright and clear and she had a keen sense of humor. She and Midge had been friends ever since Midge was small enough to enjoy riding the iron deer that guarded the Wentworth lawn. And Midge always made a point of stopping in to see her every week or so, since Miss Tess was unable to set foot outside her house any more.

When Midge told her about noticing the old car in the carriage house the day they had decorated Brose's car, Miss Tess nodded. "Yes, of course, I remember it. Papa bought it in 1919, the year after the war ended."

"Almost forty years old," Midge murmured wonderingly.

Miss Tess nodded. "Yes, it must be. I haven't thought of it in years. And, of course, I haven't been in the carriage house for a very long time. I suppose I really should get a junk man in to get rid of all that old equipment."

"Not a junk man!" Midge objected. And she went on then to explain to Miss Tess about Bob's ambition to have a real old car to work on and how they were so hard to find. "Why," Midge finished, passing along to Miss Tess some of the information Bob had given her, "there are regular clubs of people who have fixed up old cars and keep them in running order. It's a sort of hobby."

"You don't say!" Miss Tess shook her white head in surprise and made a little clucking noise. Then she told Midge, "But, my dear, your friend may have the car if he'd like. You must tell him so."

"You mean you'd sell it to him?"

"Sell?" Miss Tess smiled. "Why, no, I meant I'd give it to him, of course. It's worth nothing to me. It doesn't even have any sentimental value, as the surrey does, because Papa drove it so seldom."

Midge thought for a minute. Then she said, "I don't think you should do that, Miss Tess. I don't think it would be good for Bob."

"You don't?" The old lady's brows lifted inquiringly.

Midge shook her head. "The thing is, it wouldn't have the right effect on someone his age to find he could get something that's so vitally important to him for nothing. He'll appreciate it more if it costs something."

The wrinkles at the corners of Miss Tess' bright eyes seemed to deepen. "You may very well be right, my dear," she nodded. "How much do you think I should charge him for it?"

"Well," Midge said thoughtfully, "he's got eighty-five bucks saved up. He told me so. Why don't you charge him a hundred?"

"But if he only has eighty-five," Miss Tess objected, "wouldn't it be better if he could get the car for—say—a little less?"

"A hundred will make him reach a little," Midge said. "His dad will loan him the extra fifteen if necessary, and that way, acquiring the car will be a big, important step to him, not just something he was able to do without much effort."

Miss Tess said, "That's very perceptive of you, dear. I should have seen it myself."

And so, with Midge in the role of go-between, the deal was worked out. Bob was in a seventh heaven of delight over acquiring the old car, which proved to be a 1919 model Marmon. The afternoon before the Heydons were going to leave for Green Lake, Bob inveigled Midge over to see how he'd already begun to clean it up. With a can of brass polish in one hand and a soft cloth in the other, he moved around his treasure almost reverently, pointing out its many fine points. And Midge nodded and exclaimed admiringly. Actually, she could see that there was a certain charm about the antique chassis, the leather seat cushions and wire-spoked wheels.

"And when I think," Bob said fervently, "that if it hadn't been for you I'd never even have known about it, much less been able to get my hands on it—well, I just can't tell you how much I appreciate it, Midge."

She smiled at him. "That's okay. I'm glad it worked out."

"I've been trying to think what I could do for you," Bob told her, "so you'd know how grateful I am. And you know what?"

Midge shook her head wonderingly.

"When school starts this fall," Bob went on seriously, "I'll take you to every single thing that comes up—the games, or plays, or dances—anything!"

"Now wait a minute," Midge objected. "I'm not going to pin myself down to any long-term agreements like that."

"Oh, you needn't," Bob assured her. "You're free as air to date anybody you want to. But if you *don't* get asked to anything you want to go to—well, all you have to do is let me know and you've got yourself a date for it. See what I mean?"

"Gee," Midge murmured, her eyes lighting, "that's a pretty good proposition, Bob. I just might take you up on it sometimes."

"Feel free," Bob said, "any time. I'm at your service."

"Well, thanks," Midge said.

After all, if no one else asked her out, she might be

glad to fall back on Bob on occasion. Even if it would be a little like going out with a brother.

"You're welcome," Bob said, bending a loving look of admiration, not on Midge but on his 1919 Marmon.

# 10

## SOMETHING NEW

THE FIRST day at Green Lake, as Midge had warned Judy, was always devoted to getting the cottage into shape. This was a job no one tried to get out of, since Mom had made it clear that if she didn't get a reasonable amount of cooperation she just wouldn't come to the lake at all, when she had a perfectly clean and comfortable house in Edgewood. No one really believed she'd carry out this dire threat, but since Dad loved to fish and Midge loved to swim, they didn't care to take chances.

Judy pitched in, too. She and Midge, in their oldest shorts and tee shirts, their heads tied up in scarves to keep the cobwebs out of their hair, swept and scrubbed and dusted along with Midge's parents until the house looked clean and livable. When the last Navajo rug had been spread and the last crisp curtain hung and enough dishes and silver washed to be ready for dinner, everyone heaved a sigh of relief.

"I, for one," Dad said, mopping his perspiring forehead and dropping onto the slip-covered couch, "am going to take a nap."

Midge said hopefully, "If there isn't any more work to do, how about Judy and me going for a swim?"

"Oh, yes, let's!" her friend exclaimed.

Dad said, his eyes closed, "Ah, to be young."

And Mom nodded, smiling. "You'll have plenty of time before dinner. Poor Judy hasn't even had a good look at the lake yet."

In Midge's bedroom, as they peeled off their clothes, Judy asked, "Shall we wear our old suits or our new ones?"

"Our old ones," Midge decided. "There probably won't be anyone down at the beach this late in the afternoon. Let's save our new ones for tomorrow."

Their older suits, Midge's a pale blue and Judy's yellow, weren't too beat up for both girls to look very pretty and trim, walking down the sloping path to the beach. Through the thick trees and shrubbery, they could glimpse the greenish-blue water. And Midge sniffed appreciatively the familiar, indescribable lake smell. Far out was the deep green blob of Gull Island, where Tobey and Brose and a crowd of their friends had got marooned one rainy night and scared everyone half to death, for fear their boat had capsized. Memories came crowding up in Midge, mostly happy ones. She looked forward to coming back each year, to spending long lazy days in the sun and water, to renewing old friendships and making new ones.

The sand of the beach felt hot under her bare feet now and the water beckoned ahead. "Last one in's a dirty dishrag," Midge called, tossing aside towel and beach coat and starting to run.

Judy ran, too, laughing and eager, and they both reached the water at the same time. Midge took a flat surface dive and started swimming, while Judy shrieked as the cold water splashed her. But a second later, she submerged, too, and together, their crawls matching smoothly, they swam out toward the old white-painted diving raft. They reached the float at almost the same instant and clambered up the ladder to flop down, wiping the water out of their eyes with their palms and pushing their wet hair back from their faces.

"That was fun!" Judy exclaimed. "The water's wonderful."

Midge nodded. "Really makes you feel alive, doesn't it? Like a new woman."

Of one accord, they turned over onto their stomachs and lay there, looking back toward the beach. As Midge had expected, it was almost deserted. There was a woman sitting on a blanket, reading, while several children played nearby in the edge of the water. A couple of ten-or-twelve-year-old boys floated in inner tubes, pushing and splashing each other. Side by side on the sand a little farther up the beach lay a young man and a girl, looking deeply into each other's eyes, oblivious of all else.

"I warned you," Midge said, "that hardly anybody swims this late in the day. The busy times are around ten or eleven in the morning and from one or so until three in the afternoon. But I wanted to get all the dust of housecleaning washed off. We don't have to stay down long."

"Oh, I love it," Judy said. "I'm so glad you got your folks to bring me along."

"So am I," Midge grinned. "At least, we can console

each other if it turns out that there are no interesting boys around."

"Oh, there will be," Judy insisted. "I just feel it in my bones."

"I hope your bones are right," Midge murmured, her tone absent. She was staring back toward the shore, not at the stretch of beach they had just left, but farther along, at a point a considerable distance off. "That's funny," she said and frowned.

"What is?" Judy's glance followed hers curiously.

"There's a rope stretched out there—see?"

"Yes," her friend answered. "It seems to be fencing off some sort of private beach. See, there's another rope at the other end—'way down there." She pointed.

Midge's frown deepened. "That's funny," she said again. "Nobody ever ropes off their beach here at Green Lake. It's just open shore line all the way around. I wonder—" she broke off to think for a moment. Then she exclaimed, a little note of excitement in her voice, "Why, that's the Hawk's Rest beach! But if they have it shut off that way, they must be operating that resort hotel now!"

"What are you talking about?" Judy demanded.

Hawk's Rest, Midge explained, was an enormous old Victorian-type mansion, with oodles of rooms and extensive grounds. It had dominated the Green Lake shore from its hilly vantage point for more years than she could remember, most of the time empty and rather forbidding. Some people named Fletcher owned it first and then they all died and left it to a relative named

Claypool, who was an artist and a bit odd, but definitely attractive.

"My sister Tobey had quite a crush on him one summer," Midge remembered, "and Brose was burned! Anyway," she went on, "this Claypool sold the place several years ago and there's been talk the past few summers about it being remodeled and operated as a hotel. And I'll bet it is finally, or why would they rope off the beach?"

"Ooooo," Judy squealed. "That sounds fabulous! And shouldn't there be more boys at a regular resort like that than there'd be just living in the cottages?" she asked hopefully.

"I don't know," Midge admitted. "Could be, I suppose."

She and Judy lay on the raft a while longer, staring toward the roped-off beach. No one was swimming there now, or even lying on the beach. And the bright red diving float, anchored some distance out in the water, was deserted, too.

"You'd think somebody'd be around," Judy said wistfully.

"Probably," Midge suggested, "everybody's inside, getting all dressed up for dinner. You know how much time people spend changing their clothes at resort hotels. And speaking of dinner—" she pushed herself up.

Judy nodded, rising briskly, too. "I'm practically starved. Race you in."

Midge won, but by no more than a couple of strokes. She and Judy splashed up onto the sand together. The woman, who was still reading on her blanket, while her children built sand castles near the water, glanced up and smiled in friendly recognition. "I thought it was you, Midge," she said. "But you raced by so fast before, I wasn't quite certain. How are you? Did you just get here?"

"I'm fine, Mrs. Martin," Midge told her. And, "We only came this morning." She introduced Judy, then asked curiously, "We were wondering about Hawk's Rest. What goes on there?"

"You won't believe your eyes when you see it!" Mrs. Martin exclaimed. "All the changes—" she broke off then to call to one of the children, "Patty, don't go in any deeper. Dry off now. We have to get back to the cottage soon."

"What sort of changes?" Midge queried.

"Oh, they've really done a job on the old place," the woman informed her, "although they've managed to maintain the Victorian atmosphere quite well. The dining room is called the Gay Nineties Room and the waitresses are got up like Gibson girls, with blue-and-white-striped uniforms and frilly aprons and big white bows on their hair. They're all college girls, I understand."

"It sounds terrific!" Judy exclaimed.

Midge asked, "But can just anyone go there? I mean is the dining room run exclusively for guests of the hotel or can anyone eat there?"

"Oh, the Gay Nineties Room and the snack bar are open to everyone," Mrs. Martin said. "Of course, they charge outrageous prices, but the hotel guests don't seem to mind. And it's been well-filled all summer. The people who operate the place seem quite friendly and pleasant to us cottagers."

"The way they have the beach roped off," Midge said, "made me think they were trying to keep everyone away, except the people who are staying there."

"Oh, it's not that." Mrs. Martin shook her head. "I think that's just a precautionary measure, so their guests will know where the deeper water is. And they have a life guard on duty. I suppose he couldn't keep track of everyone if there weren't some boundaries."

Midge's and Judy's glances met meaningfully. They lingered a little longer, discussing the new hotel with Mrs. Martin. Judy remarked innocently that it must require quite a staff to take care of a place like that. And Mrs. Martin rose to the bait accommodatingly with the statement that there were more boys around than you could count—bus boys, bell boys, boys to care for the grounds.

Again Judy's and Midge's eyes flashed secret messages. Then Midge reminded her friend that it was getting late, that they should be returning to the cottage. Mrs. Martin concurred and got to her feet to begin rounding up her protesting brood.

The two girls waved good-bye cheerfully and started off along the path. "Did you hear what the woman said?" Midge asked.

"A life guard," Judy murmured dreamily.

"And all those other boys to do chores," Midge exulted.

Suddenly Judy's ecstatic look faded. "But there are the waitresses," she wailed.

"College girls," Midge said, "would be too old to bother with bus boys and bell boys—I hope."

Over dinner, they passed along to Midge's parents all the exciting information they had gleaned.

Mom shook her head, smiling. "It just doesn't seem possible, a fancy resort hotel right here on plain old Green Lake."

"I don't think much of the idea," Dad said a shade glumly. "Next thing we know, the Lake will be getting so civilized a person will have to dress up instead of being comfortable. And when that day comes, I for one will pull up stakes and get out. The main charm of the place has been its simplicity."

"But Hawk's Rest is cultivating the idea of simplicity," Midge pointed out. "Mrs. Martin said she saw one of their advertising folders and it was all about getting back to the calm life as our grandparents lived it, away from present-day pressures, and just having a quiet and restful vacation."

"It won't be as quiet and restful around here as it has been," Dad insisted. "Trust them to see to that."

"Now, Henry," Mom chided good-humoredly, "you shouldn't run the place down sight unseen."

"I'm not running it down," Dad denied. "I merely intend to ignore it. Does anyone have any objection to that?"

Midge said, "Not if you don't mean we're supposed to ignore it, too. Judy and I are planning on going over to their snack bar for a soda later this evening. It sounds so exciting, we're dying to see what it's like."

Dad shook his head, grinning. "There's no accounting for tastes. We come up here for the quiet life and right away you want to go out looking for excitement. But I don't care."

"Of course, we don't care," Mom agreed. "That is," she amended, "so long as you aren't planning on going until after we do the dishes."

"How could you even think such a thing?" Midge asked in a tone of mock hurt, jumping up to start clearing the table.

In her bedroom a little later, she and Judy had a solemn discussion as to what they should wear to go get their sodas. It was a question of considerable proportions. If they didn't change their dresses, it seemed likely they'd meet someone they would want to impress. If they did dress especially with this contingency in mind, there was a strong probability they wouldn't meet anyone in the least interesting.

"But I'd rather be prepared," Judy insisted, "even if it does turn out that we're just wasting our time."

And Midge nodded in complete agreement.

She put on a white scoop-necked blouse and a full yellow-flowered skirt, while Judy donned a pink sheath dress with little bows on the shoulders. They looked each other over critically before starting out and found the effect satisfactory.

"Don't forget the flashlight," Dad suggested, "so you can see where you're going. The road's dark." He was sorting his fishing tackle, intending to get an early start the next morning.

"And don't be late." Mom smiled at them. "It's been a pretty hard day, with the long drive up here and all the cleaning."

But Midge didn't feel in the least tired, nor, she was sure, did Judy. On the contrary, she felt light and airy and filled with a dreamy expectancy. Who could tell whom they might meet, or what lovely thing might happen, in the snack bar of a resort hotel?

# 11

## SOMEONE EXCITING

THE SNACK bar had two entrances, an outside one from the hotel's broad terrace, and an inner one from the ornate, deep-carpeted lobby, with its dazzling crystal chandelier and richly carved woodwork. Not without some trepidation, Midge and Judy chose to use the lobby entrance. This afforded them a chance to see more of the hotel itself and the guests. Several groups of people sat talking and laughing on the deep couches and comfortable chairs, a few others clustered around the magazine counter. They appeared to be pleasant people, well-mannered, soft-spoken and nicely dressed in smart pastel dresses and light-colored sport jackets.

"But they're all so middle-aged," Midge murmured to Judy.

And her friend nodded and whispered back disappointedly, "There isn't a soul near our age."

"Maybe you have to be old to afford to stay here," Midge suggested.

"But couldn't some of them have children?" Judy queried.

They continued their leisurely tour of inspection, arm in arm, pausing to admire paintings, framed in heavy gilt, and exquisite pieces of statuary in effectively lit niches. They took in every detail as they made their way toward the lobby entrance to the snack bar. But the youngest people they saw were a girl and man who appeared to be in their mid-twenties, hovering interestedly over a display of earrings in the gift corner.

However, when the two girls reached the snack bar and perched on red-topped stools at the long, gleaming counter, things began improving almost at once. The juke box was playing a brand-new tune, the lights were brighter and the voices younger and a bit louder all about. Teen-aged couples occupied several of the booths, intent only on each other. And in the large corner booth a group of girls no older than Midge and Judy surrounded a young man who was dividing his lordly favor impartially among the lot of them.

"Ooooo," Judy whispered, nudging Midge, "look at him!"

Midge nodded. It wasn't even necessary to turn around. The mirrored wall back of the soda fountain took care of that. The boy holding court didn't look a day over seventeen and, even seated, he was obviously tall. His blond hair was bleached almost white by the sun and his tan was impressively dark in contrast. Midge's heart quickened to see the way his muscles bulged under his white tee shirt.

"Now aren't you glad we dressed up?" Judy murmured.

"Um-hum," Midge agreed with feeling. And she added, her voice soft, "He looks like a Viking."

She could just see him standing straight and proud in

the prow of one of the old Norse sailing ships, the salt spray wet on his face, while he urged his men on to greater feats of exploration and discovery. Leif Ericson, she thought dreamily, might have been one of his ancestors.

"Viking, schmiking," Judy said. "Look at that bunch of adoring females around him. The competition must be rough."

"Probably," Midge said ruefully, "we wouldn't have a chance."

They sat in silence for a moment, just looking into the mirror.

"What'll you have, girls?" a dry voice intruded on their bemused reverie. "Or did you just come in to palpitate?"

"Why—I don't know what you're talking about!" Midge exclaimed indignantly, glaring at the hitherto unnoticed figure in white jacket and cap on the other side of the counter.

And Judy said with equal indignation, "Of course, we want something. I—I'll have a double chocolate soda."

"Make mine a sundae," Midge said. "Butterscotch."

"Maybe I'll have a sundae, too," Judy wavered.

"Okay, girls, make up your minds." The boy pushed his jaunty cap a trifle farther back on his close-cropped dark head and grinned at them. "But take your time." He leaned his elbows on the counter in an attitude of patient waiting. "We don't close till ten."

"Well, you needn't be so nasty!" Midge flared at him.

He was tall. That was the only point in his favor. He had a pleasant enough face, trimmed with freckles, and gray eyes that might have been attractive without that teasing, sarcastic look in them.

"I'm always nasty," he informed her. "It's my nature. You'd know that if you weren't new around here. Everybody loves me anyway, though, because even if I am nasty, I'm cute. So people make allowances. And you might as well start making allowances, too, because you're going to find that even if you fight against it, you'll eventually find me pretty lovable. So what kind of a soda or sundae did you finally decide on?"

Midge was smiling by the time he finished and Judy was laughing. "You're just crazy," she accused. "That's your trouble."

He fixed her with a reproachful glance, then turned to Midge. "Don't let her say that about me," he begged in a low, intense tone. "Because besides being nasty and lovable, I'm sensitive, too. Tom Brooks is really sensitive —any of my friends will tell you that. So what's your name, now that we're getting to know each other?"

His smile seemed a bit less sarcastic to Midge now, or else she was just getting used to it. And he was pretty amusing, even if he couldn't compare in looks with the blond boy over in the corner. He might be fun to know, just for kicks.

Judy said, not waiting for Midge to answer Tom's question, "I'm Judy Allen and she's Midge Heydon."

"Hi, Judy. Hi, Midge," Tom Brook's grin widened. "Welcome to Hawk's Rest."

"Well, thanks," Midge said. "But we're not staying here."

"Her folks have a cottage down the road," Judy supplied.

"We've been coming to Green Lake for years," Midge said.

"Old settlers, eh?" Tom chuckled. "Maybe you should welcome me. I never laid eyes on the place till I got this job at the hotel a month ago. And speaking of jobs, shall I concoct something for you?"

"I told you," Midge reminded, "I want a butterscotch sundae. How about you, Judy?"

"I guess I'll stick with double chocolate," her friend decided.

While the boy behind the counter prepared their orders, Midge flicked a surreptitious glance toward the mirror. The lively group in the corner seemed to be having a grand time. No wonder, she thought, with such a terrifically attractive boy in their midst. True, there was only one of him, to divide among five girls. But none of them seemed to mind.

She hadn't realized Tom was aware of her wandering attention until he said, "His name is Lex Gresham, short for Alex, I believe. He's seventeen, six feet one, a life guard here at the hotel and Heaven's gift to girls on the side. Any more questions?"

"I didn't ask a thing!" Midge denied, coloring.

"Say, you can blush!" Tom grinned as he set the sundae and soda in front of them with a flourish. "I thought it was a lost art."

Midge sat there, glaring helplessly. There was no use denying it, when her cheeks felt so hot. She hated and despised Tom Brooks. How had she ever imagined he had a sort of cute grin?

"I gave you each an extra cherry," he said gently. "Aren't you even grateful?"

"Gee, thanks," Judy said, laughing.

But Midge said nothing at all. She took a spoonful of her sundae and ate it miserably. It could have been sawdust.

"Don't be sore," the boy in the white jacket coaxed. "I shouldn't tease you. I don't know you well enough yet. Go on and admire Muscles Gresham all you like, I won't say another word."

"You needn't say another word to me," Midge said bitterly. "Because I won't answer you."

She proceeded to eat her sundae in stormy silence.

Tom Brooks addressed himself to Judy. "She's sensitive, too, isn't she?" he asked. "Just like me."

"You're about as sensitive as a walrus, I imagine," Judy laughed.

"And how do you know walruses aren't sensitive?" he asked. "The funny way they look, with those moustaches and all, they're bound to be."

Midge felt a smile pull at the corner of her mouth and resisted it firmly. Still, how could you stay angry at such a crazy character?

Just then the outer door to the snack bar swung open and Roger Creighton, a boy Midge had known for many summers, came strolling in. His lean tanned face lit with recognition at sight of her and he came up and sat down on an adjoining stool, asking how she was and when she'd arrived.

Midge told him and introduced him to Judy. Tom and Roger knew each other, so the conversation immediately became four-sided. By the time Roger had ordered a limeade and finished it, he and Judy were gabbing away like old friends. Their interest in each other was immediate and unmistakable and Midge felt glad for Judy's sake. Tom continued to hover close by, whenever he wasn't busy waiting on someone. Each time he rejoined them, Midge brought her glance back hastily from the gay group in the corner booth, so that Tom wouldn't notice and start kidding her again.

He really wasn't so bad, when you got used to him, she decided. Only fairly good-looking, but his wit was quick and flashing. She couldn't stay mad at him and she couldn't keep from laughing at a lot of the things he said. But that didn't stop her dreaming about Lex Gresham. If he should ever notice her, really pay attention to her, it would be almost too exciting to bear. She closed her eyes for an ecstatic second at the mere thought and when she opened them Tom was looking at her with a quizzical gleam in his gray eyes. Thank goodness, Midge thought, he couldn't read her mind. Then he'd really have something to razz her about.

Roger offered to walk them home and Judy agreed to his suggestion with enthusiasm. They really made rather a cute couple, Midge thought as they all slid down from their stools. Roger was fairly blond and Judy so dark. And he was a good three inches taller than she, which made him just about Midge's height. He hadn't grown a bit since last summer.

Tom, who had been busy at the opposite end of the

counter, came back just as they were starting to leave. "Maybe I'll see you around tomorrow," he seemed to be addressing all three of them. "I'm off duty in the morning."

Midge let Roger answer. "Sure," he agreed, "we'll probably all be in swimming if it's as hot as the forecast promises."

They left Tom, leaning his elbows on the counter, grinning.

Midge walked ahead with the flashlight and let Judy and Roger follow on their way back to the cottage. The moon was higher now and the breeze had cooled perceptibly, as it always did around the lake at night. Someone was having a beach party down near the water. You could hear voices and laughter and people singing to the faint plink-plunk of a ukulele.

Suddenly Midge felt a bit lonely. Behind her Judy and Roger were talking animatedly. Already they seemed like a couple. But here she was, all alone really. Not that she cared, she assured herself. It was just that if Judy and Roger were going to get vitally interested in each other, she was going to be in the way, unless she found someone to go around with, too, so that they could have double dates. . . .

Wouldn't it be wonderful, she dreamed as she walked along, if Lex Gresham had really noticed her tonight? Maybe he'd go up to Tom later and ask him who that girl at the counter had been.

And Tom might answer, "Which one? The little dark one?"

And Lex would say, "No. I mean the other one, the tall one with the sort of reddish-blond hair."

Tom would tell him her name then and maybe pass along the information that her family had a cottage down the road and that she was going to be around the whole month.

And Lex would sort of smile and wonder why he should feel so excited and strange over a girl whose face he had only caught a fleeting glimpse of in a mirror. And he'd tell himself not to be foolish, she was just another girl and there were more girls than he needed hanging around him already. But he wouldn't believe it. Not for a minute. He would know there was something wonderfully different about this girl, different and intriguing. And he would begin devising ways and means to meet her. . . .

"Hey, Midge," Judy's voice jerked her abruptly back to reality. "You're going past your cottage. Here's the path and your folks have left the porch light on for us."

So they had, Midge realized, retracing the steps she had taken past the perfectly familiar entrance. She said, "I guess I'm getting absent-minded in my old age."

But a little smile curved her mouth. It had been worth it, she thought, to have those extra seconds for dreaming.

# 12

## MORNING SWIM

THE NEXT morning Midge, along with several others of her usual summer crowd, lolled on the diving raft, busily catching up on all the things that had happened since they were together last. Judy and Roger splashed around in the water like a pair of porpoises. They seemed quite as taken with each other as they had been last night. Or even more so, Midge thought, observing them.

The float jiggled as someone dived off and chill water splashed Midge. She'd only been out on the raft a little while, but her suit was practically dry. It was very warm, even out here on the water. Pretty soon she'd want to dive in again and cool off. In and out, hot and dry, then cool and wet—that was the pattern. She turned over onto her stomach and just then a dark head appeared over the edge of the raft and a pair of gray eyes blinked at her.

"Hi," Tom Brooks greeted. "Room for one more up there?"

Several voices were raised in welcome, drowning out Midge's surprised, "Why, sure."

Tom clambered up the ladder, tall and thin and brown in bright-flowered Hawaiian trunks, the dark hair on his legs plastered against the skin, his black crew-cut glistening with water. He stood over Midge, deliberately dripping, until she pushed him away.

"You stinker!"

"You shouldn't get all dried off like that," he retorted. "It's too tempting."

He sat down beside her and dangled his feet in the water.

"How come you're here," Midge asked, "instead of down on that fancy new float at the hotel? Or can't the help use that?"

"Sure we can," Tom told her. "The management doesn't mind and the guests are very democratic. Only trouble is, there are five females to every male and I'm scared. I tell you, it's rough."

"I'll bet," Midge said drily. "Lex Gresham seems to thrive on it, though."

She looked off up the beach to where Lex sat like a king on his tall life guard stand. All around him was a cluster of girls in bright bathing suits, a shifting, but never lessening, crowd.

"Girls," Tom said, "are that guy's life blood. He couldn't survive without 'em. Set him down somewhere without a gang of adoring females to hang on his slightest word and he'd wither and die. The more the merrier, as far as he's concerned. Then we have," he beamed, "other guys who are—shall we say—more selective?"

"Such as you?" Midge couldn't help smiling back at him.

"Sure," Tom answered. "I'm a red-blooded American boy. I like girls, too, but one at a time, so I can really appreciate them. I enjoy intelligent conversation and who ever heard of six or eight girls talking intelligently all at once?"

"You mean," Midge asked, "that Lex is always surrounded by a crowd? Doesn't he ever have a date with just one girl?"

"Infrequently he condescends to," Tom admitted. "But she must either be lousy-rich or as beautiful as a movie starlet. Now I," he continued, his tone mock-serious, "consider money unimportant and starlets inane, with their plucked eyebrows and open mouths."

"And that's why you're here, because I'm so poor and ugly?"

"I didn't say that," Tom objected. "You've got nice long legs and you talk intelligently. And I happen to like tall girls with minds."

"Gee, thanks," Midge murmured. "I'm overwhelmed."

"What is Midge a nickname for?" he queried.

"Marjorie."

"I sort of thought so," he nodded. "You know what Midge means, don't you? A gnat."

"I know," Midge told him resignedly, "but I've been called that practically since I was born, so I doubt I could change it now."

"Would you like me to call you Marjorie?"

"It really doesn't matter," she said. "I'm used to Midge."

"Marjorie sounds more tender," Tom said thoughtfully. "Maybe I'll just call you Marjorie in our tender moments."

"What a line!" Midge laughed. "And you talk about Lex."

"I wish you could keep your mind off him," Tom said sadly. "I told you I was sensitive. You're hurting my feelings."

"Sorry," Midge said, jumping up.

She curled her toes around the edge of the float and dived in, striking the water with scarcely a splash. A moment later Tom cleaved the water nearby with even less displacement.

"Race you," he said, coming up close beside her.

"Where to?" Midge queried.

"The other float."

"Won't they care?"

"Nah," Tom assured her. "I told you the management's broad-minded."

They started off together, but although Midge did her best to keep up, Tom outdistanced her easily. Every now and then he stopped and trod water for a few minutes, waiting for her.

"Show-off," Midge accused.

"I just don't want you to drown." He grinned. "I have better ideas for our future."

"I can swim that far easily," Midge told him. "You needn't wait for me."

"I'm companionable," he said.

After that, he stayed just a few feet ahead, matching his easy crawl to hers. It wasn't really a race at all. When they reached the gaily painted hotel float, they found it was deserted except for a middle-aged couple who greeted Tom by name and smiled in friendly fashion. Most of the hotel guests were splashing about in the water much nearer the shore, or stretched out on the sand in the shade of big beach umbrellas, blooming like giant flowers in the sunshine. Around the life guard's seat the girls still clustered.

"Long live the king," Tom said drily, noting the direction of Midge's glance. "If anyone was ever actually in danger of drowning, they probably couldn't attract his attention."

Midge objected. "He must be competent or he couldn't keep his job."

"Well, we haven't had a drowning yet. But nobody's had to be rescued, so it's hard to tell."

"But he can swim, can't he?" Midge asked. "Without a life preserver, that is?"

"Okay," Tom said with a grin. "I guess I deserved that. Oh, he's got a flashy crawl all right. And he shows up fine at beach parties, too. He sings and plays a ukulele and all the girls swoon."

Midge said, "You've really got a thing about him, haven't you? Can't we talk about anything else?"

"Sure," Tom agreed, "if you'll stop looking at him like a dog with his eye fixed on a juicy sirloin. That gives me a complex."

Midge said, "You can really be very nasty, can't you? Do you take lessons or does it come naturally?"

"Now you're mad, aren't you?" Tom said.

"Yes."

"I could apologize," his tone was thoughtful, "but it wouldn't mean much because I'm not actually sorry for anything I said."

"So don't apologize," Midge said.

"Okay, I won't," Tom agreed. "Let's just talk about other things and forget there's anyone else around. We'll forget Mr. and Mrs. Wallace are over there on the other side of the float, dunking their toes in the water and we'll mentally erase all those people back on the beach and all that gang down around the other diving raft—"

"You mean," Midge put in, "we're alone on a desert island?"

"Or, hey!" Tom exclaimed. "We could be two brave explorers in outer space, heading for the first landing on the moon."

"Oh, I like that." Midge found herself smiling in spite of her firm intention not to be amused. "Let's."

"Okay." Tom nodded solemnly. "We're alone in this rocket and suddenly it strikes me that I know nothing whatever about you. And vice versa, of course. So how about filling in a few details?"

"Such as?"

"Well, I know you're Marjorie Heydon, nicknamed Gnat—I mean Midge. And I know your folks have a cottage here. So tell me everything else, please. Age, what year in school, hobbies, interests, all that junk. Then I'll tell you about me."

"It sounds utterly fascinating," Midge drawled.

But, the funny thing was, it turned out to be a most interesting morning. Later, telling Judy about it, as they were getting out of their wet bathing suits in Midge's bedroom, Midge admitted as much.

She said, "I was determined to dislike him, not for any very good reason actually, but just because he's so much less attractive than Lex."

"But he can't help that," Judy objected, tying on a

red-and-white-candy-striped halter. "You shouldn't hold it against him."

"I know," Midge said. "But can I help it, either, if the mere sight of Lex, whom I haven't even met yet, makes me feel all warm and quivery inside?"

"You felt that way over Johnnie Randall," Judy reminded. "And look how he turned out."

"Lex may be the same type as Johnnie," Midge admitted. "The way the girls hang around him makes me think so. But I'm not sure. After all, it's not his fault he's so good-looking. And I'm certainly getting a very biased picture of him from Tom."

Judy giggled. "Tom can't stand him because he thinks you're interested in him. And Tom's so interested in you."

"He likes my mind." Midge grinned. "He said so."

"Well, what all did you learn about him?" Judy pressed. "I'm dying to know."

"He's almost seventeen," Midge told her. "Goes into his last year at high school in the fall. Lives in Indianapolis, plans to go to Purdue. Has a couple of older sisters. He plays basketball, likes to swim, is interested in the hotel business, which is why he got a job at Hawk's Rest this summer. In addition to working at the fountain, he's a bus boy in the dining room. Does that answer your question?"

"Yes." Judy laughed. "It doesn't sound as if he held back anything."

"Oh, he was very frank," Midge admitted. "And he wanted to know all about me, too. Then, besides personal details, we discussed the U. N., foreign aid, whether

Volkswagons or Renaults are better, how silly it is to go steady and miss all the fun of circulating, whether rock-n-roll's fading fast and just a wee smattering of modern art."

"Wow!" Judy said. "No wonder you didn't turn up till almost noon. I'd have been worried when Roger and I got back to the raft, but the other kids said you'd gone off swimming with Tom."

"And speaking of Roger," Midge said, tying a green scarf around her slightly damp pony-tail, "how was your morning?"

"Lovely," Judy said dreamily. "Just lovely. He's really awfully nice, don't you think?"

"Sure," Midge agreed, "he is nice."

"And cute, too." Judy hugged herself.

"We-ell, sort of," Midge teased.

"You're just prejudiced," her friend accused, "because he isn't six feet tall. He has the nicest eyes and his hair's sort of curly when it's wet and he likes all my favorite T-V programs."

"What more could you ask?" Midge ducked the pillow Judy heaved at her.

Actually, she was very pleased about her friend and Roger Creighton. Judy was lucky to find someone she liked so well, so quickly—and someone who apparently liked her, too.

Tom Brooks, Midge reflected, seemed to like her well enough. If she could just return his interest, she'd be in the same pleasant situation as Judy. But it wasn't quite that simple. Not while the dazzling Lex Gresham hovered enticingly on the edge of the horizon.

# 13

## MEETING

THE DAY Midge actually met Lex Gresham
started out a little differently than any other.
The sun splashing across her bed awakened
her and she stretched and sat up and wrapped her arms
around her knees for a moment's enjoyment of the
early morning sounds. Beyond the open windows the
lake murmured gently on the shore and birds sang their
never-failing welcome to the new day and leaves made
little whispering noises as the breeze stirred them. A
glance at the clock showed Midge it was barely seven,
by far the earliest hour at which she had awakened during
their week's stay at the lake.

Energy and vitality seemed to surge through her,
bringing with them an unwillingness to linger in bed
even a moment longer. She would get up and take a walk
along the beach, she decided. She loved to do that,
savoring the coolness, the chill wet sand beneath her bare
feet, the soft sounds of a woodland world awakening.

Midge got out of bed quietly and put on her clothes,
black skinny-pants and a striped tee shirt with long
sleeves, since the beach would be cool at this hour. She
brushed her hair back and fastened it with a silver clasp.
On her way out, she paused in the kitchen long enough

to grab a couple of doughnuts, just so she wouldn't starve before she got back. Then she slipped out silently, leaving the sleeping cottage behind her.

It was a magic just-past-dawn world in which she found herself. No human sounds at all, just water lapping and leaves stirring and birds singing their hearts out. Midge made her way without crackling a twig down the sloping path toward the shore. A mist like gray chiffon still lingered along the edges of the lake and the sun made a gold-paved path across the water. Midge stood for a time, drinking in the still loveliness. You couldn't see a cottage from here and, by turning her head just a little, she could shut out the sight of the diving raft. Maybe, she thought, Indians had stood here long ago, looking out across the water just as she was doing, hearing it whisper as the little waves rippled in, feeling the nearness of the woods behind them.

She let her thought drift away, soft and indistinct as the mist that shrouded the shore, and started walking up the beach, just beyond the reach of the little waves. The sand was cool and hard beneath her feet. Some sort of gray water bird swooped low, then climbed again into the clear sky, its flight smooth and effortless and infinitely graceful. Midge's throat hurt a little with the loveliness of the hour and her surroundings. Or was it a sense of loneliness that caught at her, a feeling of smallness and unimportance in the midst of the green quiet? A curious shaped stone, rust-red in color, caught her eye and she stooped to pick it up. It felt cold and hard and smooth against her palm.

She walked along the shore for a mile or more before

she turned back. Now the cottages she passed, hidden by trees though they might be, were beginning to give off sounds of life and she no longer had the morning world to herself. A screen door slammed. There was a sound of children's high-pitched laughter. Someone was starting breakfast and the good rich bacon and coffee smell pleased Midge's nose and made her aware that two doughnuts weren't a very substantial breakfast.

As she crossed the beach that bordered the Hawk's Rest grounds, she heard masculine voices and glanced up in surprise to see Tom Brooks and Lex Gresham, in swimming trunks, approaching along the boardwalk that led from the hotel to the beach.

They saw her at the exact instant she saw them and Tom exclaimed, his glance widening in surprise, "Well, hi! What are you doing out so early?"

"I could ask the same thing," Midge countered.

"We're going swimming," Tom said. "You don't even seem to have that good an excuse." He remembered then, "Oh, Midge, this is Lex Gresham. Midge Heydon, Lex. I don't think you two have met."

"No, we haven't," Lex said. "Hello, Midge."

His eyes, Midge observed, as she responded rather breathlessly to his greeting, were very blue, like clear water. They seemed to look deep, deep into hers, with an expression of warm interest. His smile was as attractive as that of any movie star she could remember. And his physique was terrific, making Tom look thinner and more gangling than ever by comparison.

"Too bad you haven't got your suit on," Tom said. "You could join us."

"Sure, you could," Lex agreed.

Midge asked, "Do you two often go swimming so early?"

Lex said, "It's the only chance I get. I have to stick close to shore when I'm on duty, otherwise some dear little brat might lose his water wings and I'd have to save him."

"Besides," Tom said, "he can't fight his way through his crowd of adoring admirers later in the day."

Midge thought Lex might take exception to Tom's tone. But he grinned and agreed, "You're not just kidding. I never saw so many lone females as there are around this place!"

Tom reminded Midge then, "You never did tell us what you're doing out so early."

"Taking a walk," she admitted.

"A walk?" Lex repeated as though he'd never heard of such a thing.

"Sure," Tom said. "You do it with your feet, first one and then the other."

"Okay, funny boy." Lex frowned at him. He looked back at Midge then. "But all by yourself, early in the morning? I don't get it."

"I do," Tom told her. "I like to walk, too. And early in the morning the landscape's not all cluttered up with people."

Midge smiled at him. "You have the whole world to yourself."

Lex shook his head. "Sounds crazy."

"Ignore him," Tom told her. "Next time you feel a yen for a dawn stroll, let me know. I'll join you."

If it had only been Lex who said that, Midge thought. They talked for a few minutes longer, then Midge started on, explaining that she had to get back in time for breakfast. The two boys dropped their towels a moment later and sprinted across the sand toward the water. The black head and the blond one moved smoothly out toward the float, their crawls matching. Then Lex pulled a bit ahead, but Tom soon overtook and passed him. Was he showing off for her benefit, Midge wondered? If so, she wouldn't give him the satisfaction of standing around to watch. She didn't care a hoot which of them was the faster swimmer. Her fingers caressed the odd, rust-colored stone she had picked up and put into her pocket. She would keep it always, to remind her of the day she had met Lex.

Later, lying on the beach with Judy, Midge said, "It seems almost like fate for me to feel like getting up so early and then running into them as I did. Now that we've met," she murmured dreamily, sifting sand between her fingers, "I have the strangest feeling that something's going to come of it."

"You mean he may get interested in you in spite of all those other girls that hang after him? Why do you think so?"

"I don't know," Midge said. "It's just a feeling. Maybe it was the way he looked at me. Those blue eyes! And that hair!" She sighed.

"Roger is very attractive, too," Judy said. "And you know Tom said Lex uses peroxide on his hair to keep it real light."

"I don't believe it," Midge said.

"But why should Tom lie? You know he said he saw the empty peroxide bottle right in Lex's room."

"Peroxide," Midge reminded, "has other purposes than just as a bleach. Maybe Lex had a cut finger or—or a blister or something of the sort. Tom doesn't know everything."

"He'd have had to have several injuries," Judy replied, "to use a whole bottle. There isn't any doubt, though, that Tom wants to put Lex in the worst light possible with you. That's because he's so gone on you himself. Anyone can see that."

"We're just friends," Midge said. "That's all."

"Maybe that's all you are," Judy insisted, "but Tom would like to be more than that. Aren't you the least bit interested in the poor guy?"

"Well, of course," Midge admitted, "I think he's very nice. It's just that Lex is so much nicer."

"Honestly," Judy said resignedly, "you're nuts. You always get madly interested in someone who doesn't even know you're alive. The way you flipped over Pete Morrison at school last year. And him captain of the football team and a senior! But the guys who *like* you— well, take Bob Pierson back home and Tom up here—you can't see for dust. It's crazy!"

Midge said, "Any more advice to the lovelorn, Miss Allen? You should write a column."

"I'm sorry," Judy apologized. "But if you're going to moon over Lex all summer and ignore Tom—"

"I don't ignore him," Midge denied. "We're perfectly friendly. But I can't help it if he doesn't exactly send me, can I?"

"I suppose not." Judy sighed. "Still if you encouraged him just a little bit, he'd probably ask you out and we could have a double date."

Judy had a date with Roger almost every evening now and Midge supposed it did make her feel a little queer to go off and leave her hostess at home. But she assured her friend airily, "You needn't worry about me. If I get desperate enough for a date, I may encourage Tom. But I haven't reached that stage yet."

When Judy and Roger went off for their moonlight walk along the beach that evening, with the intention of stopping at the Hawk's Rest snack bar afterward for a soda, Midge stayed in the cottage with her parents. Both Judy and Roger had told her they'd be happy to have her come along, but Midge could see their hearts weren't in the invitation—particularly Roger's. So she had declined with thanks and the rather lame excuse that she had to wash her hair. Having stated this intention in her parents' hearing, she felt she had to follow through on it, although actually her hair did not need it at all.

When she came back into the living room, her wet head wound in a bath-towel turban, Mom glanced up at her curiously. "I thought you just washed your hair a couple of days ago," she said.

"The lake water makes it stiff," Midge explained.

It was such a convincing excuse, she almost found herself believing it. And her mother seemed quite satisfied. The three of them sat for a while, Mom reading a magazine story, Dad intent on the financial page of the evening paper, Midge putting polish on her toenails.

The radio was turned on, low and unobtrusive. Now and then some night bug thumped against the screen.

Mom closed her magazine and sat for a moment, staring at Midge thoughtfully. Then she said, "Judy seems quite interested in Roger Creighton."

"Um-hum," Midge agreed. "And vice versa."

Mom said, with a faint smile, "The only trouble is, her going off with Roger leaves you at loose ends. I thought she'd be more company for you here at the lake."

"She's company enough," Midge said. "Neither of us would want to interfere with the other's dates. That would be silly."

"I suppose it would," her mother said.

Midge was aware of the sympathy in her voice, but she steeled herself against it. Anyone could get a date if she didn't care who took her out. If you wouldn't compromise on anyone less wonderful than Lex Gresham, it might take longer to achieve your goal, but it would be worth it. Midge felt very sure of that. So sure that she was willing to spend some lonely evenings, waiting for Lex to realize they were meant for each other.

But what if he never realized it? a small, clear voice within her inquired.

Lex, Lex, Midge thought. *You just have to see that. It's so very plain to me.*

"Well," Mom said briskly, "so long as you're through with the paper, Henry, how about the three of us having a mad game of Scrabble?"

"Okay," Dad agreed amiably. "Get the board, Midge."

As she went in search of it, Midge thought that there

must be some inaudible, invisible, but unfailing way in which her parents could communicate. Else how would both of them have known at the same instant that, unless some diversion were suggested, she would begin to sink into a mood of despondency and end up feeling sorry for herself?

# 14

## A WALK IN THE RAIN

MIDGE and Tom and Judy and Roger had just finished a hot set of table tennis in the Lake Club rec room. They had relinquished their table to some waiting players and gone out onto the porch to catch their breath. Judy and Roger, having lost, were going to have to buy the drinks for them all. They took orders, then went inside to the fountain to get them, while Midge and Tom dropped down onto a couple of rustic chairs.

The rather ramshackle clubhouse of the Lake Club, usually deserted at this midafternoon hour, was popping with people and activity. There was a simple reason for this. It was raining. And on rainy days there wasn't much to do around Green Lake, so everyone congregated at the clubhouse.

There was a big, brightly colored poster in the lounge advertising the Midsummer Dance, which was scheduled for a couple of weeks hence. Midge had noticed it when they were inside and the thought had occurred to her that if, by some miraculous circumstance, Lex should ask her to the dance, it would make an absolutely perfect climax for their stay at the lake. Not that there seemed even the slightest chance of such a thing happening. Still, a girl could dream.

Actually, she knew, there was a much greater likelihood that Tom might invite her. The thought was not in the least distasteful, just infinitely less stirring than the idea of going with Lex. But Tom was fun, she reminded herself. She really enjoyed his company. It was strange how far they had traveled into friendship during the ten days or so since their first meeting. The complete ease and understanding between them might more likely have been based on years of acquaintance.

Her thoughts broke off as Judy and Roger came up with their drinks. Tom said, "It's about time! I thought you'd ducked out the back way or something."

"There's a mob in at the fountain," Judy declared as Roger pulled up a couple more chairs. She added, "We were talking to Betty and Chuck. I think they've been having a fight, don't you, Roger?"

He nodded, taking a long swig of his drink. "She's probably sore because he spent so much time yesterday showing that new girl, Rita, how to do a half gainer."

"That's the trouble with going steady." Tom wagged his head. "A girl begins to think she owns you."

"And vice versa," Midge agreed. "Why, at our school some of the kids act like old married couples, they're so tied down to each other."

"At my school," Tom said, "if you ask the same girl out three times, everyone assumes you're going steady whether you are or not. So then none of the other guys asks her for a date and you begin to feel like a heel not to keep on seeing her, even if you aren't very interested. I think the whole business has got out of hand."

"Who started it, I wonder, the boys or the girls?" Midge mused.

But no one knew the answer to that. "I guess it just grew," Roger said. "We had a unit on it last year in our Family Living course. They say it's based on a craving for security. There's a big trend that way in other things, too. Like college graduates looking for jobs with a company that has a good pension plan and all that instead of taking more adventurous jobs, where there's a bigger chance to get ahead, but not as much stability."

Tom said, "I get a little sick about all this yen for security. Sure, it's more bother to scrounge around for a date on a Saturday night, maybe call two or three girls. But, gee, where's a guy's sense of curiosity? If he's going steady, it'll be the same girl every time and that could get pretty dull."

Judy put in, "But look at it from the girl's angle. She may get tired of the same boy all the time, but still that's better than no date at all for school dances and things."

"Is it, though?" Midge argued. "I read an article by some psychiatrist and he said the whole idea is wrong. He said it's like little kids playing house and that it limits people's contacts and their opportunity to learn to get along with different types of personalities. He said at a time in their lives when they should be broadening their friendships, they're doing just the opposite."

"But, you know, Midge," Judy reminded her, "almost

all the juniors and seniors who are anybody at Edgewood High go steady."

"That's it!" Tom pounced. "The whole thing's based on conformity to the standards of the peer group—I had a course in it, too. And conformity," he went on firmly, "is the curse of present-day life. At least, that's my opinion."

"Shake." Midge thrust out her hand. "I think so, too."

As their hands gripped, Midge thought it was amazing how many things they seemed to see eye to eye on. Tom might not be as attractive as Lex, but he had a very good mind and she certainly enjoyed their conversations.

"No wonder there's so much conformity," Roger remarked. "The first thing they teach kids in kindergarten is to get along with the other kids and adjust to the group."

"Well, gee," Judy said, "it would be pretty much of a mess if they didn't teach them that, wouldn't it?"

"Sure," Roger replied, "but can't they get along without all having to be just alike? You can be different from someone and still get along with him and like him, too."

"Sure," Tom agreed, "I see what you're getting at. Look at the fads that start in high school. Some character wears white buck shoes in the winter and pretty soon everybody's got white bucks. Some girl whacks all her hair off with pinking shears and next thing you know all the girls have screwy haircuts."

"The girls?" Judy objected. "What about sideburns?"

"Now, now," Tom admonished, "let's not permit this

intellectual discussion to degenerate into a battle of the sexes. Girls and boys develop these screwy fads. I'll admit that."

"But the very first one," Midge was pursuing an idea, "the boy who wore the first white bucks and the girl who cut her hair in scallops—they were nonconformists, right?"

"Right," Tom agreed.

"So what do they do," she went on, "when everyone starts copying them and they're right back in the mob again?"

"You've got me." Tom shook his head. "I suppose the guy goes back to regular shoes and the girl lets her hair grow."

"It's a vicious circle," Roger said.

"What'll we settle next?" Tom asked.

"No, no," Judy moaned. "No more discussions."

"I know," Midge said and leaned forward in her seat. "Let's do something real nonconforming!"

"What?" Tom asked.

"Oh, go for a walk in the rain—or something."

"Not me!" Judy said firmly. "That's just crazy!"

"No, it isn't," Tom said, getting up. He put out a hand and pulled Midge to her feet. "I'm game. I like to walk in the rain."

"Oh, come on," Midge coaxed the others. "It's a nice warm rain."

But Judy shook her head and Roger shrugged and said, "There's a thin line between nonconformity and insanity, you know."

"Chicken!" Midge accused.

She and Tom walked the length of the porch and down the steps into the dripping gray world. They followed the path down toward the lake shore and stood for a little while, staring out across the water. Gray and rough under the cloudy sky, the surface was broken by little white caps. Not a boat was in sight, nor were any other people. Gull Island brooded darkly mysterious and forbidding.

"Sometime soon," Tom said, "we ought to get a gang together and arrange to have a beach party over there on the island ourselves—sometime when the weather's dependable," he amended.

"It would be fun," Midge agreed. "Who all would we ask?"

"Oh, Judy and Roger, maybe Betty and Chuck, if they aren't feuding, all the rest of your crowd. I can get some of the guys who work at the hotel, too, and they can bring some girls. The bigger the gang, the better at a beach party, don't you think?"

"Sure," Midge said. "Maybe Lex could come, too. A ukulele is always fun at a beach party."

"Yeah, I suppose so," Tom agreed with a notable lack of enthusiasm. But his interest mounted once more when they began to discuss when would be the best time to have a beach party.

"If the weather's good day after tomorrow," he suggested, "how about then? I'll have that afternoon and evening off."

"Wonderful!" Already Midge's eyes were sparkling with enthusiasm. "We'll get as many kids as we can and row over to Gull Island in the afternoon and take hot dogs and stuff for supper. There's always plenty of driftwood for a fire."

They walked on up the beach, discussing the details. After a while Tom glanced at his watch and frowned.

"Holy cow!" he exclaimed, "I have to get back. I'm on the lunch shift in the dining room today and it's almost noon."

They turned and headed toward Hawk's Rest and Midge had to hurry to keep up with Tom's long strides. On the hotel's empty beach, he told her, "I'm sorry to desert you like this."

"That's okay," Midge said. "I have to get back for lunch, too."

Tom had a sudden idea. "Why don't you and Judy come on over to the snack bar later? I'm on the fountain this afternoon and I'll treat you to a soda and we can really get the beach party rolling."

Midge's heart gave a funny little quiver. On a rainy day Lex was quite likely to be in the snack bar, too. After all, he couldn't be working. No one would swim on a day like this.

"Okay." She smiled at Tom. "We'll take you up on that."

"Swell." He caught her hand and gave it a friendly squeeze. It was the first time he had done such a thing and Midge felt a stir of surprise. He said, "See you later, then. And I enjoyed the walk."

"So did I," Midge admitted.

Tom loped off up the boardwalk toward the hotel and Midge made her way on along the beach, wrapped in a pleasant daydream. She was seeing herself in the snack bar, sitting all alone in a booth with Lex Gresham, being very gay and scintillating, while he looked at her with blue eyes warmed by admiration and liking.

He was speaking and Midge could hear his voice quite clearly as he asked in a low, personal tone, "Midge, why can't we be alone like this more often? I never really felt I knew you until just now."

"I know," Midge could hear her voice quite plainly, too. "I feel that way, too, Lex. It seems there are always so many other people around."

Now Lex was reaching out to take her hand in his under the sheltering edge of the snack bar table. Just where his unfailing circle of feminine admirers were, Midge had no idea. Or where Tom was, or Judy. Or why, on a miserable rainy afternoon, the place should be completely deserted. After all, in a daydream, one didn't have to worry about trivial details like that.

# 15

## THE BEACH PARTY

THE HAWK'S REST snack bar was crowded. Midge, coming in with Judy and Roger, saw that there wasn't an empty booth, or even an unoccupied stool at the counter. Tom noticed them and beckoned. As they made their way slowly through the crush, Midge noted with surprise that Lex, in spotless white jacket and jaunty cap, was helping Tom at the fountain. He didn't look too happy about it, though. Still, Midge supposed, when you worked at a hotel, you had to be prepared to do whatever job was assigned to you. Somehow, though, it didn't seem right for the lordly Lex to be mixing sodas.

When they finally managed to get seats at the counter, Midge, in order to make Lex's job easier, was all set to order a Coke.

But Tom said, "Have something exotic, now. I told you I'd treat you. How about a Special Banana Split?"

"Well—okay," Midge agreed. She loved banana splits.

"I'll make it," Tom told Lex. "You fix up Judy and Roger."

"If they want anything too fancy, you'll have to make theirs, too," Lex grumbled. "This isn't my line, you know."

"Oh, I'll just have a plain chocolate soda." Judy was obviously thrilled at the idea of Lex waiting on her at all.

Roger said, "Make mine the same."

While Lex rather clumsily concocted the sodas, Tom turned out a banana split that was a work of art. "There you are," he said, setting it before Midge with a flourish.

"It's beautiful," she exclaimed. And then, sampling it, "Ummm, tastes good, too."

There was to be a bridge tournament in the dining room, so the crowd in the snack bar diminished by the time Midge ate her last spoonful. Neither Tom nor Lex was very busy.

Midge got up her courage and asked Lex, "Did Tom tell you about the beach party we're planning?"

"No, he didn't." Lex leaned his elbows chummily on the counter quite close to Midge.

"I just hadn't got around to it yet," Tom muttered.

Midge said, "A crowd of us are going to row over to Gull Island day after tomorrow if the weather's good and cook our supper on the beach. Would you care to come?"

"Sounds like fun," Lex said. "I guess I can make it. I'll be free after four o'clock when the swimming's over."

"That'll be okay," Midge said. And she added, "You can bring anyone you want to, of course."

"And your ukulele," Judy put in eagerly. "I'm just dying to hear you sing, after all I've heard about your voice."

"Oh, it's not so much." Lex grinned. But you could see he didn't mean it.

They got into a discussion then of how many boat-loads there were likely to be and what they should take along to eat, besides the absolutely indispensable hot dogs.

"Judy and I can bake some brownies," Midge offered.

"You mean you can cook, too?" Lex smiled at her. "Tom's been holding out on me as to what a talented female you are."

"Oh, hers is a many-faceted personality," Tom said a shade dourly. "I've hardly begun to scratch the surface yet myself." He squirted soda into a glass with such force that chocolate splashed across the front of his jacket.

"Now look at you," Lex shook his head. "You're a mess."

"So I'm a mess," Tom agreed shortly.

Lex shrugged and turned back to Midge. "Sometimes," he said, "our friend here is a bit hard to dig. Don't you agree?"

"I don't think so," Midge said.

"You mean you understand the inner workings of his twisted personality?" Lex cracked. "How about explaining him to me then?"

It was different dialogue than she had imagined in her dreams, but no less fascinating. Or maybe it was simply that she so enjoyed talking with Lex that it didn't much matter what they said.

"Okay, doctor," Tom growled at Lex. "Cut the psychiatry or get a couch."

Late that night, when Midge and Judy were lying in bed talking over the events of the day, as was their habit,

Judy suggested, "You know why I think Tom resents Lex so? I think he's jealous."

"Of me?" Midge brushed the idea aside with a laugh.

"Sure. Why not?"

"I'm not that important to Tom," Midge argued. "If he's jealous of Lex about anything, it's probably his job. Being a life guard is so much more exciting than mixing sodas and stacking dirty dishes in the dining room."

"Do you suppose that's it?" Judy asked.

The question lingered in Midge's mind. Next morning, when she and Tom were sitting on the diving float after an early swim, she broached the subject with what she felt was infinite tact.

"Lex was lucky," she said, "to get a job as life guard. It must be awfully exciting and responsible."

"Responsible, yes. Exciting, no." Tom shook his head. "What does a life guard do all summer but sit in the sun and vegetate? Chances are, he'll never have to rescue anyone." He added casually, "I could have had that job if I'd wanted it."

"You could?" Midge's brows rose in surprise.

"Sure. But I figured it would be too boring. After all, what does a life guard need but good reflexes? I'd rather use my brain."

"Mixing sodas?" Midge's tone was dry. "Clearing tables?"

"Those are merely the mechanical angles of my job," Tom informed her. "The important thing is, I meet people, I serve them, I have a perfect opportunity to observe human nature. Who knows," he went on, "but what I may want to write a book someday? Look at the material I can accumulate at a place like Hawk's Rest. Or, if that doesn't work out, I've got a grand chance to learn the hotel business from the ground up."

Midge laughed. "Oh, be a writer! It sounds much more glamorous than running a hotel."

"I may even," Tom regarded her through narrowed eyelids, "make you the heroine of my first book. *If* I decide to be a writer, that is. And *if* you're a good sensible girl and get over your mad infatuation for Muscles Gresham."

"I'm not infatuated with him at all," Midge denied.

"Please," Tom begged. "Don't you know that people who intend to write books are always very observant?"

"They have overactive imaginations, too."

"Maybe," Tom agreed, "but I'm not imagining you have a horrible crush on Lex. It sticks out all over you. Can't you see what a phoney he is? And so conceited— why, he told me himself that if he only had enough influence to get a screen test, he could be in the movies just like that." Tom snapped his fingers.

"Well, maybe he could," Midge said hotly. "After all, he's terribly good-looking. And they say his voice—"

Tom wouldn't let her finish. "Don't you know," he demanded, "that crushes are very juvenile and a big girl like you should have outgrown them by this time?"

Midge glared at him. "You're just impossible! I don't know why I waste time with you at all!"

She jumped up and the raft jerked under the force of her dive. She swam back to shallow water and joined a crowd playing Keep Away with a big rubber ball. The physical activity should have helped work off her anger, but it didn't seem to. She was seething. What right did Tom Brooks have to tell her she was childish, that she had a crush on Lex? What business was it of his anyway?

She caught the big ball, despite the efforts of Roger to knock it aside. That was one advantage of being tall, Midge thought, as she threw the ball over Roger's stretching arms to Judy, who was up to her waist in the water. Roger went splashing off toward Judy and another, taller form stepped in to guard Midge.

"Mad?" Tom asked, his tone apologetic.

Midge's chin lifted. She didn't answer.

"Look, I'm sorry," Tom told her. "I'm apologizing."

After a second's hesitation, Midge asked doubtfully, "But do you mean it?"

"Sure," Tom said. "I don't mean I think I'm wrong about Lex. But I'm sorry I said what I did to you. After all, you have a right to like whomever you want to. It's not for me to make cracks."

"Exactly the way I feel about it," Midge agreed.

"So is it okay," Tom asked, a note almost pleading in his voice, "so long as I keep my big mouth shut about your affairs?"

Midge nodded. "I guess so."

The big ball came sailing toward her and she leaped up, stretching her arms to catch it. But Tom's palms thudded against it and it was snatched from her reach. As the game continued, Midge felt the last traces of her anger against him fade away. After all, he had apologized. And, for some reason, he was a rather difficult person to stay mad at.

Three rowboats and a couple of canoes, filled with cheerful picnickers, made the trip out to Gull Island for the beach party. The island wasn't nearly so mysterious close up, just a half mile waste of sand and scrub trees and sparse underbrush, with no human habitation about. It was a warm clear day and the late afternoon sun made the rippling water sparkle like diamonds.

First of all, when they reached the island, they grounded the boats well, so they couldn't drift off, and put the bags and boxes of food in a safe place. Everyone had worn a bathing suit under shorts or dungarees, so most of them began to peel off their outer clothes and go for a swim. Drying out afterward on the sand in the warm bright glow of the setting sun, they talked and laughed and started singing old songs to the tinkling accompaniment of Lex's ukulele. His voice, in Midge's estimation, was infinitely better than any of the others. It was a strong baritone, warm and true. She could have listened to him forever.

The red sun dipped out of sight and a single star shone in the pale dusky blue sky. It was like a theatrical backdrop accenting Lex's handsome blond head. Midge sighed, trying to fix every part of the magic moment clearly in her memory, so that she could keep it always.

Then Tom exclaimed, jumping up and showering her with sand, "Hey, let's start gathering wood, so we can get the fire going! Aren't we ever going to eat?"

Soon a great fire was blazing and sputtering and Midge

got up regretfully to do her share of the work. While the girls spread tablecloths and piled them with buttered buns and potato chips and jars of pickles, the boys cut willow twigs and peeled them. On these, as soon as the fire had died down a bit, they roasted the hot dogs.

The dusk was bluer now and lights had begun to flicker on in the cottages over on the mainland. Tom brought Midge a smoking weenie, burned black on the outside just as she liked them.

"You want strawberry pop or root beer?" he asked her.

"Strawberry," Midge decided.

While Tom went for her drink she doused her hot dog with mustard and relish and enfolded it in a bun. She had just opened her mouth to bite into it when, to her complete astonishment, Lex came up with another weenie for her.

"Oh, too bad," he said and smiled. "You've already got one."

"Thanks, anyway," Midge murmured.

Tom was some distance off at the moment, getting bottles out of the portable cooler. Lex dropped down on his heels beside her and Midge felt her heart beating in slow, enchanted rhythm. Lex Gresham, actually cooking a weenie for her, seeking her out, despite the older girls, the infinitely more attractive girls who were here.

Lex said, "Tom sure sticks around you. I never have a chance to get acquainted."

Midge heard her own voice with a curious detachment, saying teasingly, "Tom sticks around. What about that harem that usually surrounds you?"

Lex laughed. He had a wonderful laugh, low and

personal, as though he and Midge shared a delightful secret. "Oh, those," he said. And shrugged slightly, as though they weren't of the least importance to him. He asked then, his blue, blue glance thrillingly direct on her face. "Has he got you all dated up for the Midsummer Dance at the club next week end?"

For a moment Midge couldn't speak at all, then she gulped in a slightly chokey tone, "No. No, he hasn't yet."

"Good," Lex laid his tanned hand briefly, excitingly on hers. "How about going with me?"

"Why—sure," she managed to say. "I'd like that."

"It's a date then," Lex said. He stood up, smiling down at her, as Tom approached with two bottles of strawberry pop and a paper plate full of potato chips. "See you," Lex said as he drifted off.

Never in her whole life had Midge felt so happy. She gave Tom the widest, warmest smile imaginable as he said, "Here you are," and dropped down beside her.

She took the bottle he proffered and helped herself to a handful of potato chips. She bit into the hot dog she had just been starting to taste when Lex had come up to her so unexpectedly.

"How is it?" Tom asked. "Done enough?"

"What?" Midge murmured absently.

"Your hot dog." Tom frowned.

Midge stared at it questioningly. "What about it?"

"What's the matter?" Tom asked. "You got water in your ears or something? Can't you hear?"

"Of course," Midge said. Her glance at Tom was patient and pitying. He just wasn't one of those lucky people for whom dreams came true. But she was, so she could afford to be magnanimous. She told him sweetly, "I guess I was just thinking of something else when you spoke. I'm sorry."

# 16

## BOYS ARE CONFUSING

I STILL can't believe it," Midge told Judy as they were getting ready for bed. "But he asked me. I know he did. A person couldn't just imagine a thing like someone inviting her to a dance, could she?" Midge's tone was anxious.

"Of course not," Judy said firmly. "Not even anyone as crazy as you. But it does seem strange," she had to admit. "He's never really paid any particular attention to you before."

"He said something about Tom always sticking around, so that we never had a chance to get acquainted," Midge recalled blissfully.

"Golly," Judy sighed, "you're lucky. I can't even imagine having a date with anyone as fabulous as Lex. I wonder what Tom will say when he finds out?"

"What can he say?" Midge murmured. "He doesn't own me. And he hasn't said a word yet about the dance."

"He will, though," Judy said. "He probably thinks there's still plenty of time. But when he finds out you're going with Lex—wowie! I can't wait for the fireworks!"

Midge felt just a shade apprehensive herself. After all, Tom held such a low opinion of Lex, he was certain to resent his interest in her. Maybe, Midge reflected, this would teach Tom not to take a girl for granted and wait until the last minute before asking for a date. He had only himself to blame, but, even so, he was sure to be angry. She shivered deliciously at the thought.

Her dreams that night were troubled, whether because of the situation she was involved in, or because of all the hot dogs and brownies she had eaten, Midge wasn't sure. But she didn't sleep well and when she wakened in the morning, it was with a curious sense of foreboding, rather than the thrilled expectancy with which she had fallen asleep. Reluctance at the thought of seeing Tom, of having to tell him she had accepted Lex's invitation, weighed heavily upon her. Maybe, Midge decided, her oddly unsettled feelings grew out of sympathy for Tom, augmented by an unwillingness to hurt him. After all, they were friends and had had a lot of fun together.

When he came strolling down the beach from the direction of Hawk's Rest in the middle of the morning, Midge watched his approach with a sort of hollow dismay. She was glad that Judy and Roger were sprawled on beach towels a few feet off. With them nearby, her and Tom's conversation couldn't get too personal.

His greeting was cheerful, his manner friendly as always. Apparently Lex hadn't told him yet. Midge felt as though she were living on borrowed time as the four of them talked for a while about nothing very important. Tom kept pouring sand on her legs until he had them practically buried.

"Now look what you've done," Midge accused. "I'll have to go in the water again to get clean and I'm almost dry."

"That's why I did it." Tom grinned. "You know I hate to swim alone. Come on."

He caught Midge's hand and pulled her up. Then, tightening his grip so that she couldn't break free, he ran with her toward the water. Midge felt herself drawn along irresistibly. He was surprisingly strong, she thought as they splashed into the lake.

Then Tom said, "Race you to the raft," and they started swimming.

Midge felt sure this was just a ruse to get her alone. For a second she considered heading back toward the beach, but there seemed little point in that. Since she wasn't going to be able to avoid Tom forever, she might just as well face the issue now.

Still, she found herself hoping that someone else would be on the diving raft when they reached it. But as they climbed the ladder a little later, she saw that it was quite empty.

*Now,* she thought, *I'm in for it. When he asks me to the dance, how shall I tell him?* A queer panicky feeling gripped her.

"Beat you again," Tom said cheerfully. "You're really not much competition."

He stretched out on his stomach on the sun-warmed boards and Midge sat beside him, hugging her knees. They talked casually, although each time Tom opened his mouth, Midge expected him to bring up the subject of the Midsummer Dance. When he didn't, she felt her earlier panic gradually turn to indignation.

*All right,* she thought, *if that's how he's going to be!* It certainly didn't matter to her if he wanted to take her acceptance for granted and wait until the last minute to ask her to the dance. His rude awakening would only be postponed longer; it wouldn't be any the less devastating. She smiled faintly, imagining how dumbfounded he'd be when he heard she was going with Lex.

Tom said, turning over on his back and looking up at her, "Our beach party was a howling success, wasn't it?"

Midge nodded. "Everyone had a lot of fun."

Then, to her complete surprise, Tom said unconcernedly, "I hear Lex asked you to the club dance."

"Why—" Midge gulped, "who told you?"

"He did," Tom answered. "I guess he was a little worried for fear I might get sore."

"But, of course, you weren't." Midge's chin lifted a little.

"That's right," Tom said. "I was going to ask you myself, but, after all, I hadn't got around to it yet, so you have a perfect right to go with Lex."

"Gee, thanks," Midge said icily.

Apparently Tom was unaware of the chill. He went on, "Knowing what a thing you've got about Lex, I'm sure you'll have more fun going with him."

Midge glared. "I have *not* got a thing about him, whatever that means."

"Oh, come now," Tom said. "You don't have to put on a big show for me. We're old pals, remember? I'm happy for you, kid. You'll be the envy of every girl there."

Midge opened her mouth to say something—but what was there to say? She couldn't tell Tom she was deeply disappointed in his attitude. She couldn't admit she had never felt quite so let down in her life. She had been imagining how hurt he was going to feel over her un-expected date with Lex. But he wasn't hurt. He was indifferent. How, Midge wondered, could you ever learn to understand boys, when their reactions were so com-pletely unpredictable?

Tom's gray glance was quizzical. "Well, say some-thing, why don't you? You're pleased about his asking you, aren't you?"

"Of course," Midge said. "Wouldn't any girl be?"

"Sure," Tom agreed. "That's what I figured. Other-wise, I should think you'd have turned him down. But then, when you looked so funny and blank there for a minute, I couldn't figure you out."

"Oh, I'm mysterious, I am," Midge said lightly. She was dying to ask whether Tom was going to the dance, but it really wasn't any of her business.

As though he had read her thought, Tom said, "I'm going to take Linda—you know, the little blond waitress who was at the beach party?"

"She's cute," Midge said. But she couldn't resist add-ing, "A little old for you, though, isn't she?"

"Oh, not much," Tom's tone was mild. "She's only nineteen." He shrugged. "Anyway, I like to dance too well to miss out on going."

"It'll be fun," Midge said. "The Midsummer always is."

She didn't add that her opinion was based on nothing more than hearsay. She had never gone; even last year she'd been so young no one had asked her. But now she was fifteen and going to the dance with the most attractive, the most popular and sought-after boy at the lake. A happy little glow warmed Midge at the thought.

During the days that followed, the dance was a frequent topic of conversation between Midge and Judy. Roger had invited Judy, of course, and at first the two girls had talked about the possibility of doubling. But Midge felt such a suggestion should come from Lex. And Lex, despite some fairly broad hints on her part, said nothing about the four of them going together.

"Maybe," Midge told Judy, "he just doesn't care for double dates. Some boys don't, you know."

"He wants you all to himself," Judy murmured dreamily. She asked then, "Do you suppose it'll be like the dances at school, where you dance all evening with the boy who brought you? Or will there be some swapping?"

Midge said, drawing on her memories of things Tobey had told her, "Oh, different boys ask you to dance. At least, it's always been that way before."

"Good," Judy said. "Much as I like Roger, I think it's fun to mix more. Sticking all evening long with the same partner isn't very exciting."

After a great deal of discussion, Midge decided to wear a white sun dress with a full skirt, which, with enough crinolines beneath it, seemed almost like a formal. Augmented by the right accessories and the tan she had managed to acquire in three weeks, it should look terrific and practically worthy of Lex, she felt. Judy chose pink cotton lace, scoop-necked and sleeveless and full enough to stand out and swish enticingly.

During the days of waiting before the dance, Midge continued to see Tom as often as ever. Their easy friendship wasn't changed at all. Tom swam with her and teased her and they talked and laughed together as before. Lex didn't seek her out especially, although whenever chance threw them together, he treated her with thrilling attention. Once, on the beach, he stood and talked to her for almost fifteen minutes. And one evening, when Midge and Judy went into the snack bar, Lex summoned them to the corner booth where he was holding court and graciously bought them sodas.

Whenever Midge thought of actually spending a whole evening in his company, of feeling his arm about her as they danced, she grew almost faint with excitement and anticipation. And she tried to store up a fund of clever things to say, so that he shouldn't be bored or find her dull. After all, she reminded herself, Tom liked to talk with her, he said she had a good mind. It was just that Lex was so wonderful, so special, he made her feel inadequate. The truth was that, deep down inside, Midge still couldn't quite fathom his asking her to the dance at all.

Finally the big day arrived, although it seemed to take a very long time to do so. After their morning swim, Judy and Midge devoted most of the rest of the day to getting ready. They washed and set their hair, fussing over it anxiously. They did and re-did their nails. They pressed out their dresses and cleaned their white slippers.

"You'd think," Dad teased them over dinner, "that you two were going to a royal ball instead of just a plain dance at the club. Why, your mother and I may look in for a little while," he told Midge. "Anybody can go, you know, who has a dollar-fifty for a ticket."

"I know." Midge grinned at him. "But it's not the dance that's so important. It's who we're going with."

"This Alex, or whatever his name is," Dad said with a faint frown. "I haven't met him, have I, Midge?"

"No, but Mom did one day on the beach."

Her mother nodded. "Yes, I remember. He's a very good-looking boy and seemed quite pleasant. Of course, I don't feel I know him nearly as well as I do Tom."

She smiled and so did Dad. Both of them liked Tom, Midge knew. He had spent enough time around the cottage for them to get quite well acquainted with him.

Midge got up and told Judy, "I think we ought to start dressing."

Mom had offered to do the dishes tonight, so they wouldn't mar their nail polish. She waved them smilingly on their way.

But Dad said wonderingly, "Get ready? It's almost two hours till eight-thirty."

"Now, Henry," Mom said in laughing reproval, "you don't get ready for a dance in just a few minutes. I can remember that."

"Women," said Dad shaking his head, "are a very strange sex. And they start being that way so young, too."

Midge heard him and smiled, but she didn't stay to make an answer. Her thoughts went winging ahead ecstatically to the moment when Lex would stop by for her. Close as it was now, it still seemed just too wonderful to be true.

# 17

## MIDSUMMER DANCE

L EX WAS almost fifteen minutes late and they were unquestionably the longest fifteen minutes Midge had ever lived through. Roger had called for Judy and they had walked off up the road toward the club hand in hand. Midge, all dressed and ready, sat stiffly on the edge of her chair, aware of voices and laughter and passing footsteps on the road outside the cottage, aware, too, of muted music from the five-piece orchestra imported by the club for the occasion. She sat there tensely, her hands clasped in her lap, aware that her parents, although they appeared to be calmly reading, shared her mounting impatience and uncertainty. She could feel their sympathy going out to her, even though no word had been spoken about Lex's lateness. Midge hoped neither of them would say anything. She certainly didn't mean to. It wasn't as if he was very late. Why, any number of things could happen to delay a person a few minutes. She was often fifteen minutes late, herself. And it wasn't Lex's fault that tonight she'd been so very prompt about being ready in order to make the magic evening that much longer.

Maybe, Midge thought, if she went casually out to the

kitchen to get a drink of water, it would indicate to Mom and Dad that she really wasn't worried at all.

"I'm thirsty," she said, getting to her feet.

Mom nodded, "That ham we had for dinner most likely."

Midge snapped on the kitchen light, turned on the faucet. Just then a jaunty knock sounded at the front screen door—tap-tap-tap-tap-pause-tap-tap. Her breath came out in a little audible puff of pure relief. Not until the second of his arrival had she been able to face the awful thought lurking in the back of her mind, the fear that Lex might have forgotten he'd asked her, or that he'd changed his mind and simply wasn't coming at all. But, of course, he wouldn't do such a thing! She had known that all along. Her heels clicked a gay little rhythm as she hurried back across the kitchen. The smile she threw her parents as she headed for the door was radiant and their answering ones looked almost as delighted.

Lex stood there, tall and handsome in an off-white sport jacket and dark slacks, his hair silver-blond in the porch light.

"Hi," he greeted Midge, his voice warm and confident. He stepped aside, as though he expected her to come right out and join him.

But Midge invited, "Won't you come in? I want you to meet my father. And I have to get my stole."

While Lex and her father shook hands and he stood talking for a few minutes with her parents, Midge got her white lacy stole and little white sequin purse from her bedroom. She took one more look at herself in the

mirror and smiled faintly. Her lipstick was still intact,
her hair in the long curly pony tail looked its shining best
and the white of her dress was dazzling against the deep
tan of her skin. She had fastened a narrow velvet ribbon
about her neck with a silver and turquoise pin. Midge's
smile widened, remembering how Brose Gilman had told
her once, "If you want to reduce a man to a quivering
jelly, just wear a black velvet ribbon around your neck.
It never fails. In fact, that's how your sister got me."

Going back to join Lex, Midge hoped the magic
worked now.

Lex didn't say a word about being late. He probably
didn't realize he had been, Midge excused him in her
thoughts. But he did murmur apologetically, as they
strolled along the moon-dappled road toward the club,
"I tried to borrow a car, but no luck."

"What would we need a car for?" Midge asked.

Lex chuckled. "You aren't going to dance all night,
are you? I figured we'd buzz somewhere later for a
bite to eat, a drink—" he shrugged—"but I guess we're
grounded."

"They'll serve refreshments at the dance around mid-
night," Midge told him. "Sandwiches and punch and
all that."

"You fracture me!" Lex laughed, as though she had
said something very funny, but Midge couldn't imagine
what. "Anyway," he tucked his hand through her arm
and she felt a delicious sort of shock go through her, "the
music sounds passable."

It sounded much better than that to Midge. And the
club looked quite unlike its usual everyday self. Pale

blue crepe paper streamers and glittering silver stars decorated the lounge, which had been emptied of furniture. The floor had been waxed to a state of shining gloss and was filled with dancers. As Midge and Lex came in, a number was just ending, so their arrival attracted more attention than it might have otherwise. Midge was aware of a little ripple, eyes lighting and heads turning toward them, and she felt an inner swell of excitement to be the focus of so much attention. Probably Lex was accustomed to it, but it was a new and thrilling experience for her. And she was vividly conscious of his hand, still on her arm, of his blond head bent flatteringly close to hers.

The music began again and Lex held out his arms and Midge went into them. He danced well, just as she had known he would. She closed her eyes and felt his chin against her hair and it seemed like a lovely dream. If only, she thought, tonight need never end.

Suddenly Midge opened her eyes, a troubling recollection gnawing at her. She had felt exactly like this the night of Alicia's and Adam's party before Tobey's wedding, when she had danced with Johnnie Randall. Then, as now, she had felt the world about her fading out, had been conscious only of the one with whom she danced. But, for pity's sake! Midge thought, Lex was nothing like Johnnie. The only thing they shared was their strong attractiveness, their ability to make a person forget everyone and everything else.

She brushed the thought of Johnnie out of her mind vigorously. Why it had intruded at a time like this, she couldn't imagine.

Of course, it would be too much to hope that she could dance with Lex all evening. They swapped a dance with Judy and Roger, then one with Tom and Linda. Tom was a good dancer, too, Midge realized as he guided her about the crowded floor.

"Is Muscles living up to your expectations?" Tom teased. "Is it all too, too wonderful?"

Midge answered, stung, "He's just fine. And it looks as if you're getting along okay with Linda, too."

"Oh, I am, I am." Tom chuckled. "If she were a foot or two taller and had anything in her head besides bubbles, we could be soul mates." He added then, his tone more serious, "You see, Linda's strictly a substitute. You're here with your first choice of a date. That makes a difference."

A warm little glow welled up in Midge at his words. But then the dance ended and after an enthusiastic spattering of applause, Lex came up to return Linda to Tom and reclaim Midge. She gave Tom a rather uncertain smile as they separated. His words would be something to think about later, when her mind and heart and undivided attention weren't focused so sharply on Lex.

After a few more dances, refreshments were served. Fancy little sandwiches, which Lex devoured at one disdainful bite, and frosted cakes and big bowls of pink punch. Lex sampled the punch and gave his considered opinion that it would make excellent mouthwash. Midge found his observation clever and amusing. She wouldn't have dreamed of admitting that she was enjoying the food and drink.

"It's a pretty corny dance altogether," Lex complained. "Strictly small time. And all these ancients hanging around.

"Let's go out on the porch," he suggested, his hand cupping Midge's elbow. "Or do they have flood lights turned on?"

Midge laughed, her heart beating faster.

The long porch that faced the lake was dim, and by no means deserted. Couples were all about, sitting on the wicker chairs and couches, or perched on the rail, or just standing close together intent on each other. There was a faint murmur of voices all about, an occasional soft laugh. From the beach below came the gentle ripple of water breaking on sand and receding. The moon made a broad white path across it and the night smelled moist and good.

"This is more like it," Lex murmured when they had found a spot near the porch rail that wasn't too close to anyone else.

Midge felt his arm go around her and she thought she couldn't breathe for the wonder of it. Lex Gresham, who could have had any girl at the dance by simply lifting a beckoning finger, standing here in the darkness with his arm around her, Midge. She let her head rest against his shoulder as she looked out over the water. She couldn't think of a thing to say, not anything at all.

Lex said, "I still don't feel I've had much chance to get acquainted with you. All I know about you is— just how you look, the sound of your voice and laugh, the way you dance."

"I don't know much about you, either," Midge

managed to murmur. "Just how you look—and that you sing beautifully—and that you'd like to get into the movies."

"How'd you find that out?"

"Tom mentioned it."

"Oh." Lex nodded. She could feel him nod, rather than see him. His chin brushed her head. He said then, his voice quite serious and oddly intent, "I know I could make the grade, too, if only I'd get the breaks. But in the movies, just as in a lot of other lines, it isn't what you know, but whom you know that makes all the difference."

"You really think so?" Midge hated to believe that. "After all, if you have talent—and you have, Lex! And if you try hard . . ."

"Don't make me laugh," Lex cut in. "Who out in Hollywood is going to know I have talent, unless it's brought to their notice? I'm figuring on going out there soon as I finish school, getting any kind of job I can. But even when you're right there, unless you know someone who'll see you meet the right people, or get you a screen test—" he said, "it's murder!"

Midge nodded sympathetically. "Yes, I can see that would help." She wondered fleetingly why he was unburdening himself to her. There was something rather strange and pointed about his confidences, a note of pleading in his tone Midge couldn't fathom. She wished there was something she could do, but there wasn't.

"You know it would help," Lex said fervently. "It could make all the difference between success and failure, between really clicking on the screen and never getting a chance at all." His arm tightened about Midge as he said, his voice low and warm, "There isn't anything I wouldn't do for a person who could get me the break I need. A letter of introduction wouldn't be much trouble to write, would it, when it could mean everything to me?"

"Introduction?" Midge repeated confusedly. "I don't understand, Lex. I don't know anyone in the movies."

"Don't be modest," Lex crooned into her ear, his lips so close she felt her hair stir against her cheek. "How about your brother-in-law out in California—the producer?"

"Producer?" Midge gasped. "Oh, Lex, you're mistaken. I don't know where you ever got such a crazy idea. My older sister does live in California, but she's married to an engineer."

There was a moment's stark silence, then Lex said, "He—works for one of the studios, though, doesn't he?"

"No," Midge denied. "Oh, no, Lex. He works for a big construction company—hasn't a thing to do with the movies."

This time an even longer silence followed her words. It seemed to Midge that Lex's arm slackened its grip a little, but she might have imagined that. The music was starting up inside and the porch emptied gradually, except for a few scattered couples in the deeper shadows. But Lex made no move to go in. He said succinctly, his words spaced wide apart, "Well—I'll—be—darned!"

Midge asked, frowning, "Where did you get that idea?"

Lex's tone was curt, "Your pal, Tom, told me so."

"That my sister was married to a producer?" Midge demanded incredulously. "But—Tom knew better than that."

All the talk they had indulged in about their families, their homes, their schools. Tom knew perfectly well that Janet's husband was a construction engineer. Why, she'd even told Tom about some of the bridges Jim had worked on, the out-of-the-way places he'd been sent to.

"Of all the stinking tricks," Lex said, "giving me a bum steer like that! His idea of a joke, I suppose—him and that egg-head sense of humor of his!"

Midge moved easily out of the loosened circle of his arm. "Was that—" she managed to force the words past the aching lump in her throat, "was that why you asked me to the dance, so I'd get my brother-in-law to arrange a screen test for you?"

"Of course not!" Lex denied. "What do you think I am?"

Midge wasn't quite sure. She strongly suspected him of being a liar, an opportunist, with little regard for anyone but himself. But so great was his charm that, even though she felt sure he'd been using her, that his invitation had been motivated by Tom's fantastic tale, she still shivered with excitement when his arm went around her once more.

She turned her face aside as his mouth neared hers, though, and his lips just touched her cheek. Even so, his kiss was a stirring thing. And his husky voice, murmuring, "I wouldn't do a mean thing like that to you, baby," wasn't easy to resist.

She said faintly, "Let's go in and dance."

"Okay," Lex agreed, quite in command of the situation once more, apparently confident that he'd convinced her.

But even in his arms, moving around the floor again to the music's insistent beat, Midge couldn't put aside her nagging doubts and a hurting sense of disillusionment. Things weren't the same as they'd been earlier in the evening and no amount of pretending could make them seem so. The magic had all rubbed away. It wasn't that she was exactly angry with Lex. She supposed he couldn't help being the way he was. But whenever she thought of Tom Brooks, hot rage and resentment choked her. When she got him alone, she intended to tell him exactly what she thought of him.

# 18

## GOOD-BYE, GREEN LAKE

TOM DIDN'T join Midge for their usual morning swim the next day. "He's afraid to," Midge declared wrathfully to Judy.

"Maybe he just wants to give you time to cool off," her friend suggested.

Judy had heard, of course, all the details of the situation. And she shared Midge's resentment loyally. Still, when Midge had confided in her the night before, Judy had dared to speak up in Tom's defense, to point out that it was really rather clever of him to mislead Lex, thus giving him ample rope with which to hang himself.

Midge had been unconvinced by Judy's arguments, logical as they might be. The bald fact remained that Tom had no right to interfere in her affairs. And now, with a night's sleep behind her, she felt no less incensed at his unpardonable action.

She told Judy, "If he's waiting for me to cool off, he'll have a long wait! I feel like going over to Hawk's Rest right now and telling him off. He's probably down on their beach, afraid to show his face!" The more she thought of the idea, the better she liked it. She jumped up from the beach towel on which she'd been lying. "In fact, I'm going!"

"Gee," Judy objected, "I can't come with you right now, Midge. I promised to meet Roger here at eleven."

"It's just as well," Midge tossed back over her shoulder as she strode off. "You might feel queer, hearing me tear into Tom the way I mean to!"

Walking purposefully along the lake shore toward the hotel, Midge formulated scathing words and well-turned acid phrases in her mind. She would say this to Tom and he might answer thus. And then she would tell him such and such and he would cringe and apologize, but it wouldn't do him the least bit of good. After all, who did he thinks he was, manipulating people like a puppet master, pulling strings? Why had he imagined he could get away with it? He should have known better, knowing her as well as he did.

She must have walked very fast, she arrived at the Hawk's Rest beach so quickly. There were quite a few people about and Midge's glance flashed questingly from one group to another.

"Hi, Midge," a voice hailed her.

But it was just Lex, sitting on his thronelike chair, surrounded, as usual, by an admiring feminine crowd.

"Oh, hi," Midge answered, turning to toss him a slightly absent smile. He looked just as attractive as ever in his white swimming trunks; his blond hair glinted in the sun and his dark glasses gave him a movie-actorish look. Midge didn't recall ever having seen him in sunglasses before and it wasn't even a particularly bright day. A fleeting question brushed her mind and then drifted off. She was too intent on finding Tom to be easily diverted, even by Lex's charm. And speaking of Lex's charms, they didn't seem nearly as potent to Midge this morning, although the other girls clustering around him were obviously as dazzled as ever.

Midge felt a faint touch of pity for them. Or was it envy, because the magic hadn't rubbed thin and faded for them yet? She didn't have time to pursue the question, because just then she sighted Tom, lying alone a little way along the beach. He appeared to be asleep, sprawled on his stomach on a big towel, his black head buried in his arms. But Midge would have recognized those wild Hawaiian trunks anywhere. She went up to him unhesitantly and, stooping, tapped him on a bare brown shoulder.

Tom turned over and sat up, squinting at her. "Oh, it's you," he said.

Only he didn't say it very plainly. The words came out of his swollen, cut-lipped mouth more like "Oh, ishoo."

Midge stared at him blankly for a minute. "What happened to you?" she asked, not very brightly, because even as she spoke, the answer exploded in her mind. "You've been fighting," she accused.

"Now why would you think a thing like that?" Tom mumbled. He tried to grin and said, "Ouch," instead.

"Were you fighting with Lex?" Midge demanded.

"Then you haven't seen him?" Tom quirked an eyebrow at her. Evidently the upper part of his face worked better than his lips.

"Why, yes, but—" Midge broke off in sudden realization. "So that's why he's wearing dark glasses."

Tom said simply, "He's got a shiner that's a lulu, just in case you think I'm the only one wearing the scars of battle." He winced slightly, asking, "Could we continue this discussion in a couple of days, when my lip heals? It hurts when I talk."

"Then don't," Midge glared at him. "You needn't say a word. Just listen to me. I know you deliberately lied to Lex about me having some influence that could help him get a movie test. And I think it was a low, mean, inexcusable thing to do."

Tom said with difficulty, but firmly. "I guess it showed you the kind of a heel he is, didn't it? That's only partly what I had in mind, though. I figured you'd get a large charge out of a date with him, feeling the way you did. And how was I to know the big stupe would let you know why he was promoting you the very first time he took you out? I thought he'd use a little finesse and you'd have some fun out of it before you got onto what an egotistical phoney he is."

"But, of course," Midge said with elaborate sarcasm, "you meant for me to find that out eventually."

"A smart cookie like you would be bound to," Tom said.

"Gee, thanks," Midge murmured, feeling hot rage swell in her. "I don't suppose it ever crossed your mind that I might resent your interfering in my affairs, which are, after all, no business of yours. Such a thought wouldn't occur to you."

"Aw, don't be sore," Tom coaxed.

But Midge said furiously, "I am sore! And I intend to stay that way. Nothing you can say is going to make the slightest difference. Because I never intend to speak to you again. Is that perfectly clear? I hope I won't even see you and I'm glad we're leaving in a few days, so I won't have to!"

She turned on her heel and walked off, her chin high. If he followed her, she thought irately, she'd be tempted to hit him herself, even if he did have a cut lip. Of course, she knew she wouldn't actually do that. She had too much self-control, strong as the temptation might be. It was only boys who forgot they were civilized and descended to common brawling, as Tom and Lex had done.

But Tom didn't follow her. She had almost reached the public beach before she was sure he wasn't going to. And she was glad, Midge told herself firmly. She'd have been disappointed if he had sought to detain her. This way, she could dismiss all thought of him from her mind. Of him and Lex Gresham, too. The entire episode involving them was a closed book now and one she never intended to open. . . .

The remaining few days at Green Lake were quiet ones. Midge had expected that Tom might try to seek her out, but he didn't. She skipped her early morning swim, in order to avoid an accidental encounter. And she shunned the hotel snack bar, despite Judy's attempts to get her to go there.

"But why not?" Judy demanded. "I think you're being mean. After all, you could give him a chance to explain and apologize."

"I heard everything he had to say the morning after the dance," Midge told her. "If you think I'm going to chase him, by hanging around Hawk's Rest, you're just crazy!"

And she stuck stubbornly to her guns. Since Tom was

obviously aware, just as she was, that their friendship was over, there was no point in their seeing each other again. Midge didn't see Lex, either, as a matter of fact. He made no effort to get in touch and neither did Midge. Why should she? Lex's show of interest had been such an apparent pretense, it made her feel hot with embarrassment to think of it. For the first time in her life, though, Midge found herself actually looking forward to leaving the lake and going home.

Packing and closing up the cottage for another year had always filled her with regret before. Now she threw herself into the job with enthusiasm. Her cheerfulness annoyed Judy, who was moping over her coming separation from Roger.

Judy accused, "You act as if you're glad to leave! When I think of not seeing Roger till next summer—maybe not even then, if I don't get to come up here again—" she sighed.

"You can come again next year," Midge tried to cheer her. "Consider yourself invited already."

"But so many things can happen in a whole year," her friend moaned. "Maybe Roger and I won't even feel like this next summer. If he only lived in Edgewood —or I lived in Cleveland—"

"Cheer up," Midge said. "There are lots of nice boys back home."

"You're not helping," Judy accused darkly. "Just because you're mad at Tom and disillusioned with Lex, you find it easy to be real philosophical."

Midge said, "I'm sorry."

There wasn't much else she could say. It was true her

situation was quite different from Judy's. Midge was glad things had worked out so well for her friend. But a little throb of self-pity ached in her at the thought of her own muddled affairs.

*I guess I'm still not a very good judge of boys,* Midge reflected. Lex had turned out to be a phoney and Tom had interfered in her affairs in a way no girl should be expected to tolerate. The thing to do, she told herself, was to forget them both, wipe out the whole hateful experience as if it had never been.

Their last night at the lake, Judy went for a moonlight swim with Roger. Midge stayed at home. She was in bed when her friend got back, but not asleep.

They talked for a while, mostly about Judy and Roger, and then Judy asked, "Tom didn't drop by?"

"Of course not," Midge said. "Why should he?"

"I thought he might want to apologize or something."

"No reason he should," Midge murmured. "What good would it do? We couldn't ever be friends again, after the way he's acted. And we're going home to-morrow. I'll never see him again anyway."

She said the final words airily, but, somehow, they seemed to set up a curious chain reaction in her thoughts. She heard them echoing hollowly down the corridors of her mind. *I'll never see him again. I'll never see him again.*

She had known that all along, of course. Why should it strike her so forcibly now, just because she had put it into words?

Not that she cared at all. A dominant, interfering character like Tom. True, he had enlivened her stay at the lake with his mad sense of humor, his keen intelligence, his offbeat personality. But, certainly, she wasn't going to miss him. The very idea was absurd.

Midge smiled faintly in the darkness at its absurdity. Back in Edgewood, among her own friends, it shouldn't take her more than a week to forget all about Tom Brooks.

# 19

## HOME AGAIN

SOON AFTER the Heydons' return home, Tobey and Brose came to Edgewood for a brief visit. They had been back from their honeymoon a couple of weeks, staying in their new apartment on the Midwestern campus. Now they were returning the Gilmans' car and picking up Brose's older and less dependable convertible. They were also gathering up all their possessions that still remained in their parents' homes, wedding presents and winter clothes and the like and either packing them in the convertible's trunk, or preparing them to be sent by express to their new address.

"Honestly," Tobey said, with a rueful laugh, "I had no idea there'd be so much stuff."

"And it's such a small apartment." Brose shook his head. "I hope we can get it all in."

Never had Midge seen two happier people. Their love seemed to give them a special quality that glowed in their eyes when they looked at each other. They had had a grand time in Canada and now they were all aglow at the prospect of settling into their new home.

Tobey told Midge all about the apartment, waxing lyrical over the fact that it was newly decorated and afforded a lovely view of the wooded campus. "Of course," she added, "the closets are a joke and the kitchen's so tiny you can stand in the middle and reach everything—but that's rather handy, really."

"Besides," Brose reminded drily, "you won't have much time to cook."

"I'll have plenty," Tobey told him. "You'll see."

There was so much to talk over that time passed too quickly. The Gilmans wanted to see a lot of Tobey and Brose, too, of course. On Saturday they had a dinner party for both families. It was informal and gay. Midge would have enjoyed it thoroughly except for the haunting thought that Tobey and Brose would be leaving the next day.

Alicia and Adam came to the dinner, it being Adam's night off from the hospital. Their baby was due in just a week now and everyone watched out for Alicia and deferred to her. And she loved all the attention and practically purred with pleasure.

Midge found it hard to believe that Alicia and Adam were going to be parents, despite the obvious evidence. When the baby came, it meant she'd be aunt to three children.

"It's almost enough to make a person feel old," she confided to Tobey during their only really private conversation.

This took place in Midge's room on the morning of Tobey's and Brose's departure. Brose was loading luggage into the car and Dad was helping him. Mom was getting breakfast. As soon as they ate, Tobey and Brose would be leaving for Midwestern.

Now she said, laughing, "You're not in any real danger of that for a long while."

"Oh, I know," Midge agreed rather forlornly. "What actually worries me is how lonesome it's going to be around here."

"Don't forget," Tobey reminded, "what an utter madhouse it often was, with the four of us."

"It was fun, though—usually," Midge said nostalgically.

Tobey asked then, obviously trying to steer the talk in a new direction, "Did you have as good a time as usual at Green Lake?"

For a second Midge couldn't speak. At mention of the lake, the thought of Tom washed over her like a choking tide. *But how completely ridiculous,* she thought. *Why should it hit me that way?* There was no time just now to unscramble her confused feelings. She'd have to sort things out in her mind later, try to figure out her totally unexpected reaction.

She admitted to Tobey, "Well, yes and no," and went on to explain briefly how things had got so mixed up and all at cross purposes, with Lex and Tom both turning out so disappointing.

"Sometimes summers are like that," Tobey agreed in sympathy as Midge finished. "I can remember a few that seemed utter messes when I was living through them, although they aren't so bad to look back on." She smiled faintly, adding, "At least, it sounds as though things weren't dull for you."

"No," Midge's grin was wry, "they weren't dull."

"Hey!" Brose's voice called from downstairs. "You about ready?"

"Be right with you," Tobey called back. She told Midge, "Just find yourself someone as wonderful as Brose during the next few years and you'll be all set."

She looked so happy as she said it that Midge had to blink a little to rid her eyes of a sudden mistiness. "I'll sure try," she nodded, smiling. "Wish me luck. . . ."

After Tobey and Brose had gone, life settled down to comparative calm and quiet. But not for long. The second Wednesday in August, Alicia's and Adam's baby, a girl, was born. And on Saturday, the day before Alicia and little Anne were due home from the hospital, Mom fell halfway down the basement stairs, breaking her right arm.

Midge wasn't at home when it happened. She and Bob Pierson had been playing tennis. After their game, he treated her to a malted and then persuaded her to stop at his house long enough to see all he had done to the old car she had helped him secure. It showed the results of loving care, its brasswork polished to a fine glow and its upholstery rejuvenated. Midge even had to admit there was a certain distinction in its high, old-fashioned lines, as compared with the Pierson's long, low modern car which occupied the other side of the garage.

"And wait till you see the motor," Bob said proudly, wiping an invisible fleck of dust from a headlight with his shirtsleeve. He lifted the hood almost reverently for Midge's inspection. "Isn't she a honey? Of course, I've got lots to do on her yet, but, gee, Midge, you have no idea the way they used to build motors. It's a work of art, honest!"

Midge oh-ed and ah-ed with proper appreciation, although it looked just like any other motor to her. But Bob's delight and enthusiasm were so great she couldn't do less than hover admiringly over each spark plug and piston, just as if she knew one from the other.

"And it really runs," she asked wonderingly, "after all those years of lying idle?"

"Sure she runs," Bob said. "Of course, I've only driven her up and down the drive, but she runs real sweet. You want to try her out with me—just on the drive, of course?"

"Not today," Midge told him. "I've really got to be getting home now. It's almost dinnertime."

"I'll give you a rain check," Bob promised. "And when I'm old enough to get my license, you're the first one I'm going to take for a real ride in her."

"Thanks." Midge smiled back at him. "And we can drive the car over and show Miss Tess how you fixed it up. She was asking about it when I went to see her yesterday. But she'd get a kick out of seeing it herself I'll bet."

"Sure, we will," Bob agreed. "Just as soon as I'm old enough."

When Midge reached home, she was surprised to find the house empty. No aroma of cooking spiced the air. She couldn't understand it. Mom hadn't said a word at lunchtime about going anywhere. And even if she was playing bridge or had gone to some club meeting, she usually got home earlier than this.

Before Midge had time to get really concerned, she heard the sound of their car on the drive and went to the door curiously. Her eyes widened at sight of Dad helping Mom out of the car with the greatest solicitude, telling her gently to be very careful. And Mom was wearing a big white cast on her arm and looking quite pale and hollow-eyed.

"What happened?" Midge demanded, flying to meet them.

"I fell on the basement stairs," her mother's tone was wryly apologetic, "of all the stupid things."

"And broke her arm," Dad added.

Details came pouring forth. Mom had managed to get to the phone and had called Dad at the office. He had rushed home to take her to the hospital. Now her arm was set, there were no complications, but she'd have to wear the cast for weeks.

"And Alicia's coming home tomorrow," Mom said in a sort of wail, as Dad helped her lower herself gingerly onto the sofa. "I was planning to go over every day for at least a week and help her with the baby."

"Alicia can manage," Dad said firmly. "The doctor told you to take things easy for several days and we're going to see that you do. Aren't we, Midge?"

"Of course," Midge agreed. "I can do all the work."

"But poor Alicia's absolutely petrified at the thought of bathing little Anne all alone," Mom objected. "Of course, she has a cleaning woman and when Adam's home, he can help. But Alicia's so jittery when she's scared—"

"Stop worrying," Midge broke in, feeling a little scared herself, but not letting her tone indicate it. "I'll help Alicia."

"But—" Mom objected, "you don't know much about babies, either."

"I do so," Midge said staunchly. "We learned all that stuff when I was working for my baby care badge for Girl Scouts. We used a real baby, too. Mrs. Merton let us borrow Karen's baby brother. Of course, she came along to watch what we were doing with him. But we didn't have a bit of trouble."

"Vive les Girl Scouts," Dad said.

The little troubled wrinkle between Mom's brows had smoothed out a bit. "I suppose you and Alicia could manage together," she said. "I imagine what she mainly needs is moral support. And you could always phone me if there was anything important you didn't know."

"Of course they could," Dad told her. He leaned down and gave her a comforting hug. "Now stop all this stewing about Alicia and think of yourself for a change. Put your feet up on the couch and I'll get you some pillows and a blanket."

Midge left him fussing over Mom affectionately, tucking pillows under her arm and behind her back, and went out to the kitchen to start dinner. It was quite late, so she just heated a can of soup and scrambled some eggs and fried pork sausages. She forgot all about coffee, but both Mom and Dad assured her they'd just as soon have milk. Midge felt quite efficient and self-reliant as she went about her tasks.

The three of them ate cozily on a card table set up beside the couch, so that Mom wouldn't have to move. Her arm was throbbing quite badly now, but she was being so well taken care of, she assured them, that she scarcely minded. And the worst would be over before morning, the doctor had said.

"You'd better get to bed now," Dad told her, "and take some of that stuff he said would help you sleep."

"I suppose I should," Mom agreed. She gave Midge a warm smile. "It was a lovely dinner, dear. Thanks for taking over."

Midge said, "Gee, I haven't done anything yet. But I will."

While Dad helped Mom upstairs to bed, Midge carried the dirty dishes out to the kitchen. While she washed and dried the dishes and put them away, the silence of the kitchen made her feel a little lonely. She wished she had someone to talk to, someone to discuss her thoughts with, even someone who might join her in a good hot argument. Someone like Tom Brooks.

*But you'll never see him again,* she reminded herself, and was surprised at the thrust of pain the realization brought. . . .

# 20

## STRANGE IDEA

THE FIRST time Alicia bathed the baby, with Midge hovering helpfully at her side, it was quite an ordeal for all of them. Little Anne yelled piercingly throughout the entire procedure. Alicia's hands shook and perspiration dampened her forehead and Midge was scared pea-green, although she did her best to conceal the shameful fact. The trouble was, the baby was so much smaller than Karen Merton's little brother had been when the Girl Scouts used him as a guinea pig. And she squirmed so. Still, at last she was bathed and patted gently dry, oiled and powdered, diapered and garbed.

"I did it," Alicia breathed in a low, thrilled voice.

Midge nodded admiringly. "You certainly did."

What with spilled water and talcum and scattered soiled clothing, the bathroom was a shambles. But little Anne, oblivious to the upheaval she had caused, lay warm and clean and sweet in her mother's arms, already dozing.

"She can't fall asleep till she's eaten!" Alicia's voice held a note of sheer panic.

"Go nurse her," Midge said, "and I'll clean up this mess."

By the time she had the bathroom restored to shining order, Alicia had finished feeding the baby and was bedding her down in her pink-ruffled bassinet.

"What else would you like me to do?" Midge asked, as they tiptoed out of the nursery.

"I can't think of a thing," Alicia said. "I'm going to lie down on the couch and rest awhile. Why don't you get us something cold to drink? There's a pitcher of lemonade in the refrigerator."

Midge poured two glasses and brought them into the living room. The drapes were drawn against the heat of the sun and the soft green color of the walls gave a cool effect. The furniture was old, but good, having been bought by Adam's parents years ago. The Victorian effect was quite charming. Midge knew that Alicia and Adam had plans for a house of their own eventually, smaller and more modern than this. But until Adam's interneship was through, it worked out very well for them to live here with his widowed father.

Alicia said, as she sipped her drink, "It's really a big help having a doctor for a husband. Whenever I get panicky about anything Anne does, he'll be right at hand to tell me it's perfectly natural and that all babies act that way."

She chattered on and on about the baby. Midge got a bit bored after a while, although she didn't let it show. When a couple of Alicia's friends, bearing gifts, dropped in for a peek at the baby, Midge took advantage of the opportunity to leave. After all, Mom needed help, too. And Alicia's cleaning woman would get there by lunchtime, so she wouldn't be left alone.

Alicia offered no objection. She'd be just fine, she said.

"And thanks for coming over. In a few days I'll be able to manage alone. But right at first, it's sort of rugged."

Back at home, Midge told Mom all about the morning's happenings while they ate lunch. Mom had to laugh at her blow by blow account of the baby's bath. She was feeling better today, although the cast was awkward and she was finding out that there were a lot of things that were hard to do one-handed and with her left hand, at that.

When Judy dropped over later that afternoon, Midge was in the throes of vacuuming the living room. Judy looked trim and attractive in black pedal-pushers and striped blouse, making Midge's wrinkled shorts and soiled tee shirt seem even more dowdy by comparison.

"Poor you!" Judy commiserated.

"I'm a mess!" Midge pushed her hair back from her perspiring forehead with a grubby hand. "I helped Alicia this morning and Mom this afternoon. I expect to develop dishpan hands and housemaid's knee any time now."

Judy shook her head. "What a way to end the summer."

But Midge objected, "Oh, I was kidding. It's not really so bad. Alicia won't need help very long. She really did quite well this morning when you figure it was the first time."

"But your mother's arm will take ages to heal."

"If I broke my arm, wouldn't she do everything for me?"

"Well, of course," Judy agreed. "But I still think

it's a pretty sad way to end a vacation, all bogged down in babies and housework."

"Oh, pooh!" Midge dismissed the idea airily. "I'll have time left over for fun, too. You'll see."

As if to prove her contention, the phone rang a few minutes later. It was Bob, asking her to the movies that night.

"Why, yes," Midge agreed, giving Judy an I-told-you-so sort of look. "I'd love to go, Bob. First show? Okay, I'll be ready."

When she had hung up, Judy told her a shade wistfully, "You're lucky to have him."

"What do you mean, lucky?" Midge laughed. "I bought him, body and soul, by getting him that old car from Miss Tess."

"There's more to it than that," Judy argued. "He was interested long before the car business came up and you know it." She complained, "I haven't had a single date since we got back from the lake." And then, her tone dreamy, "Gee, I wish Roger lived here."

"You mean you liked him that well?"

"I mean because he liked me," Judy corrected. "After all, I have an open mind where boys are concerned. I could enjoy a date with anyone who isn't utterly impossible. But nobody's asked me out since we got home."

"I'm sorry," Midge murmured sympathetically. "I'll sort of hint to Bob tonight. He ought to be able to line up a double date for us some time."

"I'd even be grateful for that," Judy admitted.

After a moment's silence, Midge asked, "Do you ever

find yourself thinking of Roger and—well—missing him a lot? I mean, when something is said about Green Lake does the thought of Roger just sort of rush over you and make it hard for you to catch your breath for a minute?"

Judy considered the question thoughtfully, then shook her head. "No, I can't say it does. I miss the fun we had at the lake. And I miss Roger because he was mixed up in it. But I don't think there's anything terribly personal about my missing him."

"Oh," Midge said.

"Why?" Judy asked, her dark eyes brightening with curiosity. "Do you feel that way about someone?"

Midge nodded.

"Lex?" Judy pressed.

"Oh, no!" Midge's denial came instantly. "It's Tom."

"Tom?" Judy frowned. "But you were so mad at him."

"I know," Midge admitted. "But somehow I don't seem to feel that way any more. I just keep thinking of how interesting he was and all the good times we had together and remembering that crazy sense of humor of his—and his cute smile." She sighed.

"Gee," Judy said wonderingly, "I had no idea you felt that way about him."

"Neither did I," Midge admitted, "until just recently. And now, of course, it's too late to do anything about it."

"Maybe he'll work at Hawk's Rest again next year." Judy obviously was trying to think of something cheering to say.

But Midge murmured, "I doubt it. Boys always try

to get different jobs each summer. It's more interesting."

"Or he might write you," Judy suggested.

"Then why hasn't he done it before this?" Midge asked reasonably. "It's been three weeks now. If he wanted to get in touch with me, he'd do it right away while I'm still fresh in his mind. No, I expect he's forgotten all about me by this time."

Judy said in a low, intense voice, "I think it's terribly sad and exciting, just like in a movie. Maybe you never will forget him. Maybe the memory of him will haunt you always and . . ."

"Oh, come on!" Midge objected with an uncomfortable little laugh. "Now you're getting carried away. I'm not that big a dope."

Judy stared at Midge thoughtfully, her chin on her palm. "Do you know what just suddenly struck me?"

Midge shook her head.

"Everybody you fall really hard for," Judy pursued her idea solemnly, "is unattainable. Have you realized that? First there was Johnnie, who was 'way too old. Then it was Lex, who was so popular, you'd hardly expect him to notice you. And when Tom was right there for the taking, you didn't think much of him at all. But now that you've lost him, he suddenly seems real attractive to you."

Midge stared at her friend with a troubled frown. Put that way, it did sound like a strangely recurrent pattern. But that couldn't be it! She was sure Judy's analysis was wrong, her reasoning faulty. She told her, "There may have been some similarity in the way I felt about Johnnie and Lex. I guess I had a sort of crush on both of them. But I know it's altogether different with Tom."

Judy shrugged. "I don't see how you can be real sure about it if you never see him again. But you know what else I wonder?"

"What?" Midge asked, not at all certain she wanted to hear.

"I wonder, if Bob Pierson suddenly lost all interest and started ignoring you, if you'd begin to like him a lot."

"Now that's the silliest thing I ever heard!" Midge declared scathingly.

She wished Judy would get another boy to date. Being at loose ends gave her too much time to think about her friends' affairs and come up with utterly crazy ideas.

# 21

## SURPRISE FOR MIDGE

IDGE was glad that the remaining weeks of summer were busy ones for her. And secretly she welcomed the thought of school starting soon, because then she'd be even busier. She liked the routine of school and found study stimulating. Besides, there'd be the daily contacts with a wide circle of friends. And, as a sophomore, there'd be more clubs and activities open to her than there had been when she was just a freshman. The prospect was inviting.

It hadn't taken Alicia long to reach the stage where she was able to manage the baby's care herself. Actually her efficiency surprised everyone a bit. She settled into the role of motherhood happily and little Anne thrived. But although Midge no longer had to help Alicia, she found herself continuing to do a good deal of work at home. Mom tried to help, but her cast hampered her so much that Midge wouldn't let her.

"You deserve a little vacation," she told Mom. "Just take it easy for a while. When I'm back in school and don't have so much time it will be soon enough for you to start doing a few things."

Housework and cooking kept Midge's days fairly

occupied. She usually had some spare time in the after-noon, though, for more enjoyable pursuits. She played tennis with Judy or Bob. Occasionally Bob got another boy to make up a foursome for a set of doubles or a movie. Midge and Judy also went horseback riding whenever they could fit it in. There was a sprawling farm on the edge of town where they rented horses and both girls loved to ride.

With so many duties and activities, it seemed as if Midge wouldn't have had much time left to think about Tom. But no matter how firmly she pushed him out of her mind, the memory of his wry grin, the echo of his voice, crept back to trouble her. She'd think of his satirical humor, the fascinating talks they'd had, the way his long stride matched hers so comfortably as they walked along the shore, his endearing habit of waiting unobtrusively for her when they swam.

Why, she asked herself more than once, hadn't she appreciated him then instead of waiting till she lost him? She didn't know the answer. Still, she was sure it wasn't the one Judy had suggested.

Midge hashed the question over with Mom one after-noon as they sat on the porch, in order to get the benefit of an older, wiser opinion. She said, "I just couldn't have developed this feeling about him because he's inaccessible now. I know it."

Mom nodded, her tone serious and sympathetic, agree-ing, "I don't think it's that, either. Crushes, such as you had for Johnnie and Lex, are a part of growing up. Almost all girls go through them. I can even remember having a few myself." She smiled faintly. "But I think you're past that stage now. I expect, as sometimes happens, you just went along taking Tom for granted when he was around, not realizing how well you really liked him. And of course Lex was at hand to dazzle you, too, which probably made it harder for Tom's less obvious charm to register."

Midge guessed that was the way it had been. But somehow there wasn't much comfort in the thought now. "I don't know why I was such a dope. After all, he did me a favor, showing Lex up in his true colors. It was even sort of flattering in a way for him to get into a fight with Lex over me. I don't feel mad at him about it at all any more—but he'll never know that."

Mom said, "I'm sort of a fatalist about such things myself. I feel that if you and Tom are supposed to get together again, if you could really have a good and lasting friendship—well, things will work out so you do get together. If it's better that it all ends now, then it ends."

"Your tense is wrong," Midge corrected. "It has ended."

Somehow, though, she did feel a little cheered by her talk with Mom. Maybe next summer Tom would be at Green Lake again. She wouldn't let herself hope too hard, or count on it, but there was a possibility. The only trouble was, next summer seemed an awfully long time off. . . .

Labor Day came and went. Midge always thought of it as the end of summer, even if the calendar didn't agree. School loomed less than a week ahead now. The first Tuesday in September was a bright, hot day, the sky clear blue and cloudless, the thermometer hovering in the nineties before the afternoon was well started. Mom was taking a nap and Midge had just come downstairs from her shower. She wore crisp white shorts and a candy-striped halter and she had tied her hair high and cool with a black ribbon. Afterwards, she was to look back and feel abjectly grateful that what happened didn't happen a half hour earlier, when she was still in grubby jeans and no lipstick. But you had to get the breaks sometime!

The doorbell rang and Midge, who had been on her way out to the side porch, turned back to answer it. And there, just as he had done so often in her dreams of late, stood a tall, lanky, startling familiar figure. Stubby black hair, quizzical eyebrows, a slightly uncertain, but attractive grin—Midge's heart flopped.

"Hi, Midge," Tom said.

"Why—why—" she was too stunned, too breathless with surging happiness to speak intelligibly.

She could only reach out to open the screen door for him. And stand there, staring up at him, as he came in.

"Gee, Midge—" Tom's voice was husky and he sounded almost as breathless as she. He reached out and caught one of her hands and held it hard. "I wasn't sure if you'd let me in, but I took a chance."

"I'm glad," Midge said, hoping he'd never let go of her hand. "I've been—wanting to see you, so I could tell you I'm sorry."

"For what?" Tom's brows rose.

"Because I was such a stinker at the lake."

"That was I," Tom corrected, "not you."

But Midge shook her head, her smile radiant. "Let's not even talk about it any more."

Tom insisted though. "There are a couple of things I've got to explain. You must have wondered why I never came near you after that day on the beach when we had the argument."

"I just figured you didn't want to."

"Don't be silly," Tom said. "The thing was my uncle had forbidden me to leave the hotel grounds."

Midge frowned confusedly. "What uncle?"

"That's right," Tom nodded. "You don't know about him. I'd better begin at the beginning so you can get it all straight. Gary Deckard, who owns Hawk's Rest, is my uncle. But when he gave me my summer job, he said it would be best if no one knew we were related, so there'd be no question of favoritism. That was okay with me. I wanted to be treated like the others. Everything went fine till Lex and I had that fight. Uncle Gary was pretty burned up about the whole business and he said, if I stepped foot off the hotel grounds while you were still at the lake, he'd fire me."

Midge nodded, intent on every word, feeling like a femme fatale and adoring the sensation.

"There were a couple of good reasons why I didn't want to risk that," Tom went on. "One was that I took the job in order to learn more about the hotel business, which is the line I'll probably want to go into when I'm through college. And the other was that my uncle had promised me a juicy bonus if I worked all summer long." He admitted, "I thought of trying to sneak over to your cottage, but that didn't seem fair. And of course you didn't have a phone."

Midge asked, "Why didn't you write me?"

"I tried," Tom's tone was dry. "But I found I wasn't very good at expressing my feelings on paper. In fact, I don't seem very good at describing them in person, either. All I know is, the bottom sure dropped out of my summer after you left. I missed all those talks of ours, those walks and swims. I missed you!"

He said it so accusingly Midge had to smile. She admitted softly, "I missed you, too. And I was sure I'd never see you again."

Tom grinned down at her, squeezing her hand even harder. "Boy, I couldn't face the thought of that. Not when, by merely detouring a couple of hundred miles, I could drive through Edgewood on my way home." He pulled Midge toward the door and pointed at the car parked at the curb. It was a shining new little red foreign car which Midge hadn't even noticed until now. "In a new Renault like that," Tom finished, "what's a few hundred miles?"

"Is it yours?" Midge asked wonderingly. "It's beautiful."

"My bonus," Tom told her proudly, "from Uncle Gary. For good and faithful service all summer long. You see why I didn't want to take a chance on losing it? Not that you aren't worth it, of course. But I figured if I played my cards right, maybe I needn't lose either one of you."

They laughed together and Midge felt color creep under her skin. But somehow, she didn't even mind blushing in front of Tom. He seemed so understanding, so close, so almost like a part of her. It was a wonderful warm feeling. She hoped Tom shared it, too.

Her tone was anxious, asking, "You can stay, can't you, now that you're here? You won't have to rush off?"

"I can stay till tomorrow, if I'm coaxed," Tom assured her, "and still have plenty of time to get home before school starts."

That meant they'd have all the rest of today and some of tomorrow together, Midge added up delightedly. In that length of time she'd have plenty of opportunity to show Tom off to all her friends, to take him on a personally escorted tour of Edgewood, so he could see all the places she'd told him about. More important, it would give them a chance to get even better acquainted, to build a sturdier foundation under the wonderful friendship they'd started this summer. A friendship, Midge felt sure as she looked into Tom's gray eyes, that was going to last and last.

"In that case," Midge said, "please stay, Tom."

"Shucks, ma'am," Tom told her, "you didn't have to say 'please.' " He laughed, but there was an undertone of seriousness in his voice as he added, "You're going to find I'm a hard man to get rid of."

As if I'd try, Midge thought.